The Enemy You Know

A Psychological Thriller

TANISHA STEWART

Table of Contents

Dear Reader,

Welcome to the final installment of The Quiet Ones series. I've always wanted to write a psychological thriller, but I was searching for a source of inspiration. It finally came when Ebony Evans, founder of the EyeCU Reading & Chatting group on Facebook presented a group of authors with a challenge that she calls **Freestyle Fridays**.

In the challenge, the authors were given a theme and a set of pictures and told to let their creative juices flow. From this challenge, Shatina's story was born. You met Shatina in **Should Have Thought Twice**, but she is a different woman in *The Enemy You Know*.

Buckle up and enjoy the ride. When you finish, I would love it if you could leave a **rating** or **review**. Happy reading!

Tanisha Stewart

The Enemy You Know

A Psychological Thriller

Chapter 1

It wasn't until Sam felt her life slipping away that she realized she didn't want to die. She'd sent that last text to the crew, but as far as she knew, no one had written back. Did they not care? Why hadn't anyone reached out to her?

She was lying on her back on her bathroom floor, blood oozing from both wrists. The stinging sensation was oddly soothed by the slow, but steady stream of life exiting her body. A tear rolled down her cheek. Sam's phone lit up and buzzed, but she didn't have the strength to answer it.

Probably one of the crew, finally returning her message. Too late.

Could it be Robert?

No, it wasn't him. Robert had abandoned her, just like Dexter, and just like her biological father had done all those years ago. She was alone. She was void. She was nothing.

Weaker she became and as the moments passed, Sam knew this was it.

She had lived a short life, but at least she tried to make things right before it was over. Shatina got her sister back. Most of the crew made it out alive.

But Buster… Sam sniffled.

She didn't want her heart to go there, but it did. Didn't want her final thoughts to be of him, but they were. Buster cared for her, and she knew it.

She used him.

First, by seeking him out to exact revenge on Shatina and Max, then by sleeping with him for her own selfish gain, knowing he thought they were building toward something more.

Now, because of her actions, Buster was probably dead.

Gone.

Like she was about to be.

If he didn't make it, it was her fault.

If she didn't make it, it was her fault.

Sam and Robert didn't make it. That was her fault too.

Seth didn't make it. Sam again. If she hadn't sent that video to the chief of police, Brighton…

Sam's thoughts became faint echoes in her ears, fading from sharp focus to a faraway place.

She heard multiple voices in that place.

One of them sounded like Robert.

A faint smile crossed her lips. Or had she imagined it? She couldn't tell fantasy from reality at this point.

More muddied voices, then she was floating away.

Goodbye world, was the last thing she remembered thinking.

***

Shatina rode with Max as they raced to Sam's house, but when they pulled up, Shatina's heart dropped. There were police cruisers and an ambulance outside.

2

Shatina looked at Max, her voice trembling as she spoke. "Oh my God..." What happened? Ted said that Sam left some strange messages on his phone. Sam stormed out of Luke's house, but Shatina hadn't thought much of it at the time, figuring she was pissed about the situation as a whole and wanted to blow off steam. Never would she have thought...

But should she have suspected Sam might have been spiraling? Shatina thought back to the night they were in the limo trying to save Shatara. Sam had been crying outside the club. Then when they tried to uncuff Shatara from the chair she was in, Sam got frustrated at herself for not being able to get the cuff loose.

Then it was the fact that Sam seemed so eager to help them, to rectify what she had done by sending that video to the police...

All of it was coming back to Shatina now, painting a clear picture in her mind of Sam's mental state. Shatina didn't want to get too far ahead of herself, but she hoped Sam hadn't...

Max cut into her thoughts. "I want to go in, but I'm afraid because of the police."

"Forget the police!" Shatina said, wanting to use a much stronger word, but her fingers were already enclosed around the door handle and wrenching it open.

Max scrambled out of the driver's seat to follow suit.

As they made their way toward the chaos, Ted walked out of the house. Shatina stopped short as vomit rushed to the top of her throat. Why was there blood on his shirt and his hands?

"What happened?" she demanded in a shrill tone. Her mind began swimming. Sam wasn't... She hadn't... Had she?

Shatina couldn't take that kind of news.

Ted's eyes were glassy and he beheld a dumbfounded expression, but shook himself out of it. "She still had a pulse when they put her in the stretcher." He gestured toward the ambulance.

"What happened?" Max asked. "What did she do? Or did someone do something to her?" He lowered his tone when he said the last part, shooting a glance at Shatina.

Shatina immediately knew why. She hadn't considered the thought that Brighton might have gotten to Sam.

Ted confirmed her prior assumptions. "She slit her wrists." He spoke as if it pained him to say those words, his voice almost cracking as he continued. "She called me almost a hundred and fifty times. I should have... I wasn't..."

Now Shatina was pissed. "She called you a hundred and fifty times and you didn't answer? What the hell is wrong with you?"

Ted hung his head in shame. "We had a fight. We had broken up. I didn't..."

"You broke up?" Max shot out. "When did this happen?" He looked at Shatina, and Shatina recognized from his expression that he was putting two and two together as well about why Sam was acting strange that night in the limo.

Ted shook his head. "It's a long story, but you two need to get out of here."

"Why?" Shatina said. "We need to see Sam!"

He held his hands up to protest. "You can't. They are going to take her to the hospital, probably to a psych ward, and that's if she makes it." His tone was professional now, like he had distanced himself from the situation already.

"They have to allow us to visit her," Max said.

"Only after she's stabilized, and only if she gives permission," Ted clarified.

"Why didn't you answer her calls, Ted?" Shatina asked with accusation in her tone. She knew it was irrational to take everything out on him, but Ted was an easy target and her frustrations from the past few days had to be let out somehow.

"I'll contact you two later," Ted said, and walked toward the police officers.

Shatina watched in disgust as he began a conversation with them. "That prick!" she said to Max. "How could he just walk away at a time like this?"

Max stared at the cops, then back at Shatina. "Babe, we do need to get out of here. He's right."

"What?"

"Come on." He grabbed her arm and gently prodded her toward the door.

Shatina snapped out of it, rationalizing that their departure was for the best, especially since the ambulance was halfway down the street anyway.

She breathed a silent prayer for Sam as they made their way back to Luke's spot.

***

Shatara was sitting on pins and needles as chaos ensued inside Luke's house. Less than five minutes after Max and Shatina left, Buster's vitals began to plummet. Luke worked frantically to stabilize him, while Jared and Rambo shouted orders like they had any level of medical experience.

"Can you guys shut up!" Luke screamed, his face red from all of his efforts.

Shatara was in a desperate place. She felt a connection to Buster, though she had only just met him a few days ago. Maybe it was because her blood was flowing through his veins. He had to make it.

"Come on, Buster!" Shatara whimpered, tears running down her cheeks. Her body was shaky and her voice trembling. She began praying. "Please God, let him pull through."

It wasn't working.

Luke's heart monitor stopped frantically beeping and went to a flat line with a steady sound like the one heard on TV and in movies.

"No!" Shatara pushed Luke out of the way. She had no idea what she was doing, but Buster had to make it.

She tried CPR, though Luke had already tried that. She pumped his chest with a vengeance and parted his lips to breathe into them one more time. His mustache hairs tickled her lips, and his lips were soft and smooth, awakening parts of her that had been put on hold since long before this situation unfolded, but now wasn't the time for that. Buster had to make it. He could not leave this apartment in a bag.

Shatara scrambled on top of his body so she was straddling him, pressing on his chest from another angle, then bent down to breathe into him again.

"What are you doing?" Jared yelled. "You're gonna crush him. He got shot in the chest!"

She tried and tried, but after five minutes, it was clear her efforts were in vain.

Shatara let out a wail of anguish, then punched Buster's lower abdomen, causing blood to seep through the patch in his chest.

"Come on, honey," Luke said in a low, gravelly voice.

Shatara stared at him through her tears.

Jared and Rambo had acted like this was a source of entertainment for them, like they were on an episode of House or something, but Luke seemed to understand the seriousness of what Shatara was feeling. Another life gone. Another person who came to help her lost his life.

Her mind flashed with rage toward Shatina, but her heart became overcome with grief for Buster. He looked to be her age. She was twenty one. This wasn't fair.

Shatara allowed Luke to help her down off his body, then he hugged her and handed her a tissue for her unconsolable tears.

Esmeralda stood in shock, rooted to the same position she was in before Buster started spiraling.

She trembled as she pointed. "Look!"

Shatara and Luke whipped their heads toward Buster again.

"What is it?" Shatara sniffled, then dabbed her eyes.

"He moved!"

"What, no he didn't," Jared said, doubt covering his features.

"Yes he did!"

Rambo looked doubtful too.

They all studied Buster, but his body wasn't moving. Shatara was becoming annoyed by the sound of the heart monitor, so she ripped the cord out of the machine.

Silence filled the room.

Dreadful, painful silence.

"He moved, I swear," Esmeralda said.

It was clear none of the guys believed her. "Maybe you thought you saw him move because Shatara was on top of him," Luke suggested.

Esmeralda shook her head, firm in her convictions.

Shatara couldn't take this. She grabbed Buster's hand, which was still warm. His hand was huge compared to hers, and flashes of that night at the club went through her mind. He had died trying to save her.

"Oh Buster." She burst into a new set of tears, then pressed her head against his chest.

What the...

She heard it.

She couldn't have heard it.

Her head whipped toward Luke, then her eyes shot to Esmeralda.

"His heart is beating!"

Luke sighed, then chose a delicate tone for his next words. "Honey, that's not..."

Shatara stalked over and grabbed his hand, pulling him toward Buster while Jared and Rambo watched with intrigue.

"Feel it!"

Luke was about to protest, but everyone saw Buster's eyelids flutter at that moment.

"Buster!" Shatara screamed at the top of her lungs as Jared and Rambo swore simultaneously. "Buster!"

His lids fluttered again, then he gasped deeply.

"Gloria a dios!" Esmeralda moaned, with her hands up in the air.

Buster turned his head slightly and looked directly at Shatara, just as she fainted from the gravity of the moment.

Chapter 2

Brighton Miller stewed as he paced back and forth. This wasn't good. He just got the heat off his back, now here it was again. He had no idea how that Seth kid slipped under his radar. Now there would be trouble.

Brighton heard from McConnell that there would be a news story emerging soon about Seth's death at his club, and the story would connect Seth back to his prior case since he was supposed to be testifying against him before everything got overturned.

"Dammit!" Brighton pounded on the table in his office.

What the hell was he paying these people for, if they couldn't do the simple work he requested? Rodney was supposed to get rid of Seth the first time, but he failed. *How do you shoot someone in the head and they not die?*

Rodney was taken care of by Max and Shatina, ironically, and Brighton was one step away from pinning the murder on them when Seth returned and put him right back in the spotlight.

Brighton had to think. His clients were growing impatient. He'd been sending them a steady stream of girls, high quality, and they paid handsomely for his efforts.

If that revenue stream dried up…

A migraine was coming on. "Tony!" He barked, knowing the idiot was standing outside the door.

As Brighton suspected, Tony walked in immediately. "Yeah, Boss?"

Brighton could have done without Tony being moved up to right hand status, especially since he wasn't smart enough to move like Brighton needed. Ate was far more intelligent, but unfortunately he met his demise via a stiletto to the jugular.

Brighton let out a low chuckle. *Was it Shatara or Esmeralda who did it?* Then he sneered. Two girls were missing, and Toledo, the client who wanted to purchase Shatara, was furious.

Rightfully so, because Brighton didn't come across many young girls in this area who held the exotic level of beauty Shatina's twin possessed.

Brighton's features softened as an idea formed. Maybe there was a silver lining here…

"Boss?" Tony repeated.

Brighton sucked his teeth, irritated that Tony had interrupted his thoughts. "Get me a bottle of Tylenol, and while you're at it, send Carmen in."

Carmen was Esmeralda's sister.

Tony stared for a moment.

"Did you not hear me?" Brighton snapped.

"Okay, I got you," Tony said, then exited the room.

This was why Brighton needed a better guy to fulfill Ate's role. Where would he find another thoroughbred like that? Blue Street was full of tough guys, but how many of them had the smarts it would take to stay under the radar, especially at a time like this?

***

Max and Shatina returned to Luke's house to see Buster's eyes open and Shatara sitting next to him, holding his hand.

"Wha...?" Shatina said as she took in the scene, her eyes widening.

Max was relieved. "Thank God," he said. "I didn't think I could take any more bad news."

Everyone stared at them after that comment.

"More bad news?" Shatara asked, her eyes narrowing. "What do you mean? What happened with Sam?'

Max shot a glance at Shatina, who had to have caught the obvious accusation in Shatara's tone, as well as the fact that it was directed at her.

Shatina swallowed, but didn't answer.

"She slit her wrists," Max let out.

Esmeralda gasped, and Shatara's eyes narrowed further. "She what? Why?"

Jared stood with his arms crossed, ready to hear the story, and Rambo was leaning against the wall, also intrigued. Luke was laid out on the couch, likely exhausted from the round the clock care he had been providing for Buster.

Max shook his head. "It had nothing to do with this situation. She had a bad breakup."

Shatara snorted. "Yeah, right. Buster lying here in a pool of blood and Seth's head getting blown off inches from her had nothing to do with it, I'm sure."

Max turned to Buster, starting to get irritated by Shatina's sister despite the fact that he understood her position. "Glad to see you back man." He meant those words. Although Max had been pissed at Buster previously for how he forced him and Shatina to rob his old boss, Buster had been a solid part of the crew ever since.

The crew. Max shook his head at the thought. Who were they fooling?

"Thanks," Buster said, his voice raspy. Then Shatara lifted the cup of water she was holding to his lips. Buster took a sip from the straw and nodded.

Max contemplated the weight of the situation they were in. Half of them had no idea what they were doing, and the other half were too dangerous to trust.

Just then, Luke's front door opened. Max startled at first, then calmed when he realized it was Slim, Jared's driver. He brought in some huge bags of Chinese food and a couple 2-Liter sodas. Jared moved to grab the sodas, while Rambo went to Luke's cabinets to grab plates, cups, and utensils.

"Can we at least go see her?" Shatara's arms were crossed now, and judging from her body language, she wasn't finished digging into Shatina to make her feel bad.

Shatina opened her mouth to answer, but Max cut in again, ready to defend his woman. "No, she's not able to see anyone yet. She will probably be on suicide watch for the next few days, but hopefully she will reach out after that."

Thankfully after Max's explanation, Shatara backed down and took the plate Rambo extended to her. Max shared a glance with him when Shatara wasn't looking and nodded to thank him. Rambo smirked and handed Shatina her plate. His gaze at Shatina lingered, and for a second, it made Max tense up, but when Shatina shot him her own grateful smile, Max relaxed. The man was only trying to diffuse the tension.

***

Brighton was finalizing his new plan to get himself out of this debacle when McConnell poked his head into his office. "You got a minute?"

Brighton grimaced. "Not really." That Tylenol Tony brought did nothing for his migraine.

McConnell was still standing at the door.

"What?" Brighton shot out, exasperated.

McConnell started slowly. "I don't mean to bother you, but you're going to want to hear this."

After hearing McConnell's story, Brighton's lips turned up into a sinister smile. Just the opening he needed.

Chapter 3

The whiteness of the hospital sheets blinded the darkness Sam felt in her soul. Both wrists were bandaged, and at first it took a moment to realize why, then she remembered.

She failed.

One simple mission and she couldn't get it right.

A nurse entered her room.

"Hey there, sleepyhead!" she said in a cheery voice, causing Sam to suck her teeth.

"What time is it?" Sam asked.

"It's around three o'clock. You've been out for a while. The doctor should be in in a few moments to have a chat with you."

"Can I have my phone?" Sam grumbled.

The nurse stared at her, curiosity etching her features. "Your phone?"

"Yes. My phone." Usually Sam would try to hold more of a respectful tone when speaking to people in professional settings, but she was more than pissed off at the moment.

"Honey, I don't think I can let you have your phone right now."

"What?" Sam's voice raised an octave.

"You'll need to be cleared by the doctor first," she clarified.

"Send him in then."

"It's a she, and I will go get her now."

Before Sam could utter another word, the nurse waltzed out of the room.

Sam muttered a swear word in her direction, but she wasn't sure the nurse caught it.

Five minutes later, and no doctor had arrived. Sam sucked her teeth and moved to get out of bed and find her herself when the door opened and another woman walked in.

Sam relaxed and immediately felt more comfortable. Her doctor was Black. Not that race mattered, but that other lady was way too cheerful and it was comforting to see someone who looked like her on her care team, or whatever this was.

The doctor smiled and walked over to hold out her hand. "I'm Trishia. How are you, Sam?"

Sam studied Trishia's microbraids before she let out a smile of her own and accepted the handshake. "I'm okay, I think. Sorry for yelling at the nurse. I guess I woke up here and overreacted."

Trishia paused. "Stacey didn't mention you yelling at her, but I appreciate your apology. She's one of our best."

Now Sam felt like a jerk. "Can I please have my cell phone?" she said in a low voice.

Trishia dashed her hopes. "We can't allow cell phones in the psych ward, but once we get you to a comfortable state of mind, you will be discharged to the regular hospital floor."

A comfortable state of mind? "Are you saying I'm stuck here without a phone?"

Trishia's voice was soothing, but straightforward. "Don't think of it that way. We are here to serve you while you heal mentally, then the rest of the staff will ensure your proper physical healing. Are you up for a few questions about what brought you here?"

Sam's mind flashed with pain, but she shook it off. Might as well talk if she wanted to get out of here. "Yes."

Trishia asked questions, and Sam provided answers that she hoped helped her cause.

***

Tony dipped the wash rag in the warm water, then used it to dab at Carmen's lip. She winced. There was a bruise under her left eye that made him sick to his stomach.

Everything within him wanted to kill Brighton Miller, but he knew he couldn't. At least not now. Tony needed help from the outside if he wanted to ensure his and Carmen's safety, maybe even help some of the other girls.

When Tony first linked with Brighton, he had no idea this was what he was doing. He knew Brighton's club hosted sex parties as well as other events, but he had no idea there was literal evil being performed in the lower parts of the building. When Brighton passed Tony up for Ate as his right hand, Tony was initially pissed. He had been part of Blue Street longer than Ate and done way more to earn his stripes.

Brighton didn't think Tony was the man for the job until Ate was killed by one of the girls.

Tony knew he was a sitting duck until Brighton found someone better. He had to move quickly, he just didn't know how to get in contact with Seth's ex, Shatina.

From what he knew, she was running with the crew who had successfully saved Esmeralda, Carmen's sister, as well as Shatara, Shatina's sister. If they could do all that, they might have what it takes to stop Brighton Miller's operation.

Carmen sniffled. "Where were you, Tony?"

Her words hit him like a shot to the chest. He felt like a failure. He was supposed to be protecting her while she was in here, keeping her from Brighton and his sinister ways, but he failed. Brighton had gotten his hands on Carmen and beat her because her sister escaped.

"I'm sorry baby. He sent me out on a run. I didn't know he was going to do that to you."

"Can you get me out of here?"

Her soft voice was almost too much for him. It stirred his inner loins, but it panged his heart even more.

"Yes, I'm going to get you out of here."

Tony prayed he could keep his promise. He hadn't expected to fall in love with Carmen, but he did, from the first moment he saw her.

Their relationship started slow. He would come chat with her while doing his rounds at night to check on all the girls, then it turned into something more. He and Ate were on rotation back then, and Ate never caught their stolen kisses or the night they finally sealed the deal. They had to move quickly because time only granted minutes for them to fulfill their lust for each other. Carmen's moans were soft but sounded like music to Tony's ears as he entered her, then filled her with his forceful, but gentle thrusts. Unfortunately, their lovemaking had to cease for the time being. Brighton moved Flex, another guy from Blue Street, up in the ranks to take his former position.

Tony didn't like Flex because he was down with what Brighton was doing to these girls. Tony might have been a drug dealer and a killer, but he never would do something like this to a woman.

He had to get Carmen out of here.

***

It was time for Shatara to face her mother. She would have to tell the lie of a lifetime to throw her off from what really happened, and Shatara didn't know why she agreed to it.

Part of her wanted to break down, lay in her mother's bed, and drink hot cocoa like the old days after what she had been through.

The other part knew she had to handle this situation like a grown woman. Even though she hated her sister, Esmeralda's sister was still with Brighton Miller.

Shatara had to do what it took to help her get out.

She rolled her eyes in the back seat of Max's car as that thought crossed her mind. What the hell was this? She was no action hero. Shatara was a twenty one year old college student whose life became a movie.

She couldn't believe she had almost been made a sex slave. That thought haunted her at night, and she didn't think she would ever get over it, along with all the bloodshed that occurred right before her eyes. Shatara was no gangster. She had no idea how Shatina seemed to be holding up so easily.

Who was her sister?

Shatara thought she knew her all her life, but now, she wasn't so sure.

She never would have guessed Shatina could commit a crime. Especially not involving murder and guns. And

19

before he was killed, Seth had mentioned that he was running with Brighton Miller. Was Seth secretly a gangster too? That totally threw Shatara for a loop. Seth always seemed squeaky clean, a track star who got straight A's and worked his way through college. Was it all a lie? What was the truth anymore?

They pulled up to Shatina's apartment and it was time to go inside so Shatara could get her cell phone and call her mother. She still had no idea what she was going to say without alerting her to the fact that she had somehow been involved in some of the events that had caused the city to go into a frenzy.

It was still all over the news, even though several members of the Blue Street gang were arrested in connection with the shootings. There had been no mention of the sex trafficking business though. Shatara wasn't sure if that was because the police were keeping that under wraps or because they didn't know about it.

This was a big mess.

They walked inside the apartment and Shatina handed her her phone, all charged and ready to make calls.

Shatara swallowed, then took the plunge, tapping her mother's name in the contacts. She caught a glimpse of over a hundred missed notifications before the phone began ringing.

It was cut short after the first ring. "Shatara?" Her mother's shrill voice sounded over the phone.

Shatara put it on speaker, afraid to hold this conversation alone.

"Yeah Mom, it's me." She forced a neutral tone.

"Where have you been? Where are you? How come you haven't answered your phone?"

Every word from her mother's mouth was like a blow to the chest. Shatara didn't know how to handle this. She should have rehearsed beforehand. What could she possibly say to calm her mother down?

She stared at Shatina. As much as Shatara hated her sister right now, Shatina knew how to lie. She'd done it for years to her whole family. No one had ever suspected what Shatina was up to, and Shatara still had trouble believing it now.

She thrust the phone in Shatina's direction for her to take over.

"Hello?" Shatina cut in.

"Shatina? What are you doing with Shatara? When did you come in contact with her?"

"I've been in contact with her, Mom," Shatina said in an even tone. "I told you that. Nothing was wrong. Shatara just took a leave of absence from school. She plans to go back for the summer semester."

"No, no, you're not going to run that lie down to me!"

A video request showed on the phone and Max darted out of the line of vision.

Shatina looked nervous, but she answered the video call. "Mom, I'm not lying. She's right here. Shatara was staying in a hotel for a bit to figure out what she wanted to do, but she came here because she was afraid to call you by herself. She knew you would be mad."

"Let me see your sister!" their mother barked.

Shatina swallowed and pointed the video in Shatara's direction. Their mother's voice trembled as she spoke through her anger. "Girl, do you have any idea how worried I've been? How worried your father has been? Tamika and Tyonne blowing up my phone because you weren't talking to them either? Do you have any idea what we've gone through? This is why I didn't want to let you study abroad. You're selfish, Shatara! Plain selfish, and always have been! You got your sister out here hiding you and the whole time you could have just let us know you were okay. I can't believe you."

Shatara's eyes filled with tears as her mother's voice cracked.

"I'm sorry, Mom," was all she could say.

"Yeah, I bet you are!" The call ended.

Shatara drew in a breath, all types of painful emotions swirling within her. She wanted to go to her mother's house and tell her what really happened. But she couldn't. She had to be strong until this was over.

She turned to her sister.

"I freaking hate you!" she screamed, then raced to the bathroom and slammed the door behind herself.

Chapter 4

Sam was still pregnant. She found out during Trishia's line of questioning, when she asked whether she had thoughts of hurting her baby.

"Hell no!" Sam snarled, incredulous that she was asked such a question, then she calmed when she realized that if she had succeeded in her plan, her baby wouldn't have survived. "Sorry," she offered. "No, I would never want to hurt my baby. I was depressed over my breakup and some issues I was having with my friends. I don't want to harm myself any longer, and it was never my intention to hurt my baby. I wasn't thinking clearly."

Thankfully, Sam's answers seemed to work, because after three days, she was discharged to the regular floor in the hospital.

She was informed that she wouldn't be staying long - they wanted to keep her for observation overnight and then discharge her in the morning.

For that, she was grateful, but as she sat in her new hospital bed, it hit her that she was alone. Her heart panged. Did anyone know she was in here?

The door to her room opened, and one of the orderlies entered, carrying a bag containing some clothes and her cell phone. The outfit inside the bag wasn't the one she was wearing when she slit her wrists - she remembered, so someone must have packed it for her. Who packed it? Robert?

She swelled with hope, then it deflated. It couldn't have been Robert. He ignored all of her calls, texts, and voicemails.

Who then? Her mom? Was she called to the scene? What happened that day? The last thing Sam remembered was passing out.

"Can I get you anything else?" the staff member asked.

Sam shook her head, welcoming his absence when he left.

Sam picked up her cell phone with trembling hands, then sighed with relief when she noticed that the crew had texted her repeatedly.

She checked her last message to them and realized it had failed to send. That was why no one reached out to her sooner.

There was no text from Robert, but he had called.

Sam's eyes blurred. Was his call just a formality, or had he been concerned about her?

She didn't have a chance to think, because the door to her hospital room opened again, and this time, the person who entered wasn't a member of the staff. It was a man wearing all black and sporting black gloves.

Sam's heart dropped to the bottom of her chest. "What are you doing here?" She shrieked. "Nurse!"

The man held a finger to his lips. "Shsssshh." He smiled, but it wasn't the friendly kind. "I'm not here to hurt you. I came to deliver a package."

He walked over, and Sam's heart pounded with every step. Her finger was on the hospital's call button just in case. "Who sent you?"

The curve in his lips grew wider. "A mutual associate of ours."

Sam watched as he reached in his pocket and pulled out a burner phone.

Brighton, was her immediate thought. Somehow, he knew. *Damn it!* she thought, but it was bound to happen sooner or later anyway. Brighton had found out that she was working with Max and Shatina.

The man spoke again. "Our associate said that he trusts you will be around your friends again. When he's sure you are, he will reach out."

Sam didn't respond. She took the phone, knowing she had no choice not to.

"See you soon."

He smiled once again before exiting the room.

Though the man hadn't harmed her in any way, Sam couldn't get over the fact that he was able to enter her hospital room so easily.

Sleep escaped her that night.

***

You and your sister come to the house. Now.

Shatina didn't know why she thought she and Shatara were off the hook with their parents after Shatara's disappearance. Her father's text message proved that wasn't the case.

If her dad was upset, she was in trouble. Usually her dad was a man of few words who tried to be good natured and see every situation from multiple sides. Shatina should have known he wouldn't let this slide.

Shatara sucked her teeth when she read the message on her own phone. Max looked up from his laptop. "What is it?" he asked when he noticed the women sharing a glance.

"Our dad just texted us," Shatina answered. "We're in trouble. He wants us to go to the house."

Max stared. "What are you going to tell him?"

Shatina sighed. "The best we can do is stick to the story I came up with. Shatara, you were confused about your major and a little upset that Mom and Dad didn't let you study abroad, and you submitted the leave of absence in revenge."

Max didn't look convinced. "You think they'll believe that?"

"They'll have to," Shatina rationalized. "Shatara is grown, so there's really nothing they can do. They'll probably be upset for a while, but once they see that Shatara is fine they'll get over it."

"Easy for you to say!" Shatara shot out. "I can't just go in there and let a lie like that slip off my tongue, Shatina! How am I gonna convince them?"

"You have to, for Esmeralda."

Shatara shifted in her seat on the couch, then sucked her teeth. "This is so unfair."

Shatina had had enough. "Life is unfair." The words came out colder than she wished, but she was sick of Shatara jabbing at her every chance she got. "Look, I'm sorry all this happened, but I never meant for it to turn out this way. I'm just as caught up as you are, Shatara. Can you cut me a break?"

"No, I will not cut you a break!" Shatara pounded on the couch cushion as she spoke. "I asked you for weeks what was up and you lied to me! Seth was alive and you knew it! You told me you and Max were dating but made no mention of the fact that our lives were in danger. You made it seem like we were getting closer, building our bond. But everything was all a lie. You're a liar, Shatina. You need to own that."

Shatina grew hot around her ears. "I am not a liar! The only reason I didn't tell you what was going on was because I wanted to protect you. It was me and Max's lives in danger, not yours. I never wanted you involved in this."

Shatara scoffed. "Oh really? And look how that turned out. If your flimsy plan of escape hadn't worked I would be in another country!"

Before Shatina could make a move, Shatara was on top of her, pummeling her. Shatina began fighting back, and Max intervened to get the two women away from each other. It wasn't as hard to do because it was clear that neither twin wanted to hurt the other. They both were hurting internally in different ways. The fight was a way to let out their frustrations.

Shatina swallowed, wiping a tear from her face. She felt a scratch on her cheek from her sister. Shatara's lip was beginning to swell.

"Look, I'm sorry!" She croaked. "I don't know what else to tell you."

Shatara stared at her for a long time, then she stalked over to the kitchen to grab an ice cube from the freezer. Max and Shatina watched as she wrapped it in a paper towel then applied it to her lip.

She turned back to face them, the hostility still evident in her facial expression. "What are you guys waiting for? Dad said we had to come now. Oh yeah, that's right." She let out a rough chuckle. "Max, you can't come because our parents have no idea you're even associated with their daughter. Yet another secret."

"Shatara..." Shatina began, but Shatara held her hand up and began walking toward the bathroom. "Shut the hell up, girl." She slammed the door, which appeared to be her customary response to disagreements as of late.

***

While Shatina and Shatara were gone, Max contemplated his relationship with Jared. There was dysfunction there too, and it was even worse than what Shatina and Shatara were going through.

Was it though?

It pained him to admit it, and he definitely understood Shatina's side because he knew the whole story, but Shatara's words toward her sister reminded him of how he felt about Jared. Every time he let his guard down, Jared did something to make him put it back up.

Max didn't know what to think about his brother, just like Shatara didn't know what to think of Shatina.

Max knew Shatina was a good person at her core. The whole reason they were in this mess was actually his fault, not hers.

He went after her in the beginning, forcing her to help him try to kill Sam, then again when he approached her about Brighton. She played a role, but the only bad thing she'd done in Max's eyes was to try to kill Rodney for killing Seth.

Even that was understandable, because Shatina and Seth were engaged to be married before his supposed murder.

Max felt for everyone involved in this situation. They had to take Brighton Miller down for good.

Chapter 5

Shatina and Shatara wore makeup to hide the evidence of their scuffle. Shatina hoped it worked because they were already in hot water as it was.

They drove in silence on the way to their parent's house and when they arrived, Shatara was shocked to see her car parked out front.

"How did they get my car?" she asked.

Shatina turned to her. "Mom found out you took a leave of absence from school. She went on a rampage looking for you. She came to my apartment with the police and everything."

When Shatina said that last part, she knew she had let out too much. Shatara probably would have heard this news anyway, but she didn't need to hear it now after the argument they just had.

Shatara sighed and shook her head in disbelief. "Wow," was all she said, but offered nothing more.

Shatina exited the driver's side on shaky legs. She had no idea how this conversation was going to go. They had to keep their stories straight. She wanted to remind Shatara of this, but another glance in her twin's direction made her decide against it.

They walked up to the front door and their mother whipped it open before they had a chance to knock.

"Come in," she said, more of a demand than a request.

The women entered and saw their dad sitting on the couch with a stern expression on his face.

"Hi Daddy," they said in unison before sitting on the loveseat.

Shatina couldn't determine from his facial expression how this was going to go.

He assessed them both with his eyes before speaking. "Glad to see you're okay, Shatara."

Shatara swallowed and nodded. "I'm sorry for not answering your calls."

Their father nodded, his expression softening before it re-hardened. The look on his face was enough to make both women sit up straighter in their seats across from him. "Don't ever let anything like that happen again."

Shatara nodded.

Their mother sat down next to their father, not saying a word. Shatina could tell she was still stewing from the situation.

She looked at their father, then turned to the twins to speak. "Have you watched the news?"

Shatina's heart plummeted. Why was she asking that? "Huh?" she said, playing dumb.

"Shatina, Seth wasn't dead. His funeral was a coverup for him being in witness protection. He was just killed for real the other night outside a club."

Shatina forced a look of painful surprise to her face. The surprise was fake of course, but the pain was all too real. She didn't need a reminder of what happened to Seth that night. He died right in front of her.

Her mother assessed her as if discerning something. "Did you know anything about him being in witness protection?"

"How could she, Mom?" Shatara cut in, much to Shatina's surprise. "If he was in witness protection, that meant the police kept it under wraps."

That seemed to appease their mother, and she let up.

"I hope this doesn't reopen an already gaping wound," she said.

Shatina's eyes blurred. "I'll be okay."

They stayed and talked with their parents for another hour after that. Shatara had to promise repeatedly to contact her school first thing in the morning and submit the paperwork to return to campus for the summer semester, but other than that, it appeared the issue was smoothed over.

The sisters were going to meet up with the rest of the crew at Luke's spot for updates on their plan for Esmeralda's sister Carmen's escape.

As they walked back toward Shatina's car, Shatara stopped short. "Actually, I'm going to drive myself."

Shatina froze. "Why?"

A dark look crossed her sister's features. "If I sit in your presence for another moment, I'll explode."

"Shatara..."

"I mean it, Shatina. I can't be around you unless it's about the plan. You can't just do what you've been doing and get away with it."

Shatina balked. "You really think I've gotten away with anything?"

Shatara was already opening her car door and hopping inside.

Shatina had no choice but to acquiesce to her sister's wishes.

***

Max was shocked to see Sam when he entered Luke's apartment. His eyes shot to her wrists before he could think about it, and Sam self-consciously pulled her sleeves down to cover the bandages.

"My bad," he said.

Sam didn't respond.

Buster, who was sitting up in Luke's makeshift hospital bed, was staring at Sam. "I'm glad we both pulled through."

This time, Sam did answer. "Me too."

"Awww!" Jared said in a silly voice, and Rambo pushed his shoulder. Luke looked a lot more relaxed as he battled against Slim in a racing game on the flatscreen TV.

"Come on!" Slim whined when he lost the race by a few milliseconds. "You definitely put in a cheat code for that."

Luke chuckled. "Right."

Sam was staring at Max.

"What?" he asked, his ears growing hot. He hoped that she wasn't angry with him.

"I have some news."

"What news?"

Before she could answer, Shatina and Shatara knocked on the door. Max had answered and saw both of their cars parked in the dirt driveway. *Guess they're still not on good terms.*

"Where's Esmeralda?" he asked, suddenly noticing she wasn't in the room.

Just then, she emerged from the direction of the bathroom and sat on the couch next to Luke and Slim.

Max turned back to Sam as Shatina and Shatara got settled in seats at the kitchen table.

Sam's face reddened. "I had a visitor while I was in the hospital."

"Who brought you home?" Buster blurted.

Sam looked taken aback by the question, but she answered it. "My mother. We had a long talk before I came here."

"Who was the visitor?" Max asked.

Sam drew out a breath. "Someone sent by Brighton." She pulled a burner phone out of her purse and extended it for everyone to see.

The color drained from Jared's face. "That phone came from Brighton?"

Sam eyed him. "Yeah, one of his guys brought it to me."

Jared became fidgety. "Is it on? Don't turn it on in here."

"Why not..."

"That thing could have a tracker on it!"

Sam swallowed and nodded like she understood. "I gotchu. I wasn't thinking. Sorry."

"No need to apologize but we have to turn it on away from this house. Like far away. In the woods or something. And when he contacts us, we get our own burner and give him that number. Just to be safe."

Jared was acting way too cautious for Max's liking, despite the situation they were in. "What's going on?" Max asked, eyeing his brother with suspicion.

Jared's pupils darted back and forth before he looked at Rambo.

Rambo didn't say anything, though he clearly knew why Jared was so nervous.

Max sucked his teeth. "Come on. Let's go somewhere to get a new phone, then turn that one on to receive Brighton's message."

Everyone wordlessly followed. Sam led the way to her cabin, where there were plenty of other burner phones stored. The cabin was also a location Brighton knew about, so if there was a tracker on the burner he left, it wouldn't matter. Unless he planned to bomb the place or something.

Sam looked at Max, then Jared before turning the phone on.

When the screen lit up, they saw that there was a text message sent four days ago from a private number.

Sam clicked on the message to check it, and it was a link to a video. "Doesn't he ever get any new ideas?" She wrinkled her nose. Brighton had sent them a video message last time he reached out when he kidnapped Shatara.

Before Sam could click on the message, Jared spoke up. "Wait."

Sam looked at him. "What?"

Jared turned to Max, the uneasy expression returning to his features. "Bro, before you watch that video, I have something to tell you."

***

Max grew more pissed at his brother by the second, Sam could tell.

"Are you freaking kidding me?" Max said with incredulous rage when Jared finished.

Jared gave him a sheepish grin. "Sorry bro. I didn't think things would go this far."

"Jared..." Max started, then stopped as if at a loss for words. Then he walked up to his brother and socked him in the jaw.

It looked like it hurt, but Jared didn't fight back.

He nodded, his eyes watering from the blow. "My bad, I deserved that."

Jared began walking toward the kitchen sink. At first Sam didn't realize why he was doing that but when he spit out blood, she understood.

Her eyes shot back to Max. His face didn't portray an ounce of remorse for what he had done.

Max shook his head, looking like he wanted to hit Jared again. "So you mean to tell me we're in the middle of a gang war and we didn't even know it?"

Rambo jumped in to defend Jared. "It really has nothing to do with you guys, it's more so me and Jared and our guys."

"But that doesn't matter, Rambo! Jared's my brother. I'm sure people know that by now. I'm guilty by association."

"Like I said, I'm sorry bro, but we can't cry over spilled milk." Jared was leaning against the sink, staring at his brother.

Sam could tell he felt bad, though he was fighting not to show how much.

"How long have you been down with Parker Square?" Max asked. Parker Square was a known rival gang against Blue Street. Bodies had been dropping back and forth between the two for at least a decade.

Jared held his chin up with pride. "Since I went on the inside. They held me down in there, and I do the same for them out here."

Max looked like he was putting two and two together. "That explains everything. How you came into so much power and money so quickly. How you had access to so many resources."

Jared didn't respond, but it was clear that Max's suspicions were correct.

"Let's watch the video," Sam said, trying to redirect the tension. Hopefully whatever Brighton had to say wouldn't be anything crazier than they'd already dealt with.

His ugly face filled the screen.

"Hey Sweet Cakes!" He blew an obnoxious kiss for good measure. "By now you've gleaned that I know your little secret. You crossed me. I knew it before I was released, but I let you believe I had no idea because I wanted you one more time. Hope your boyfriend enjoyed my gift." Brighton puffed on a cigar before continuing. "Anywho, this message is more for Max and Shatina. Bravo on getting Shatara and Esmeralda out of my clutches, but it looks like you left someone behind."

Brighton turned the camera so Carmen, Esmeralda's sister could be seen tied to a bed, writhing back and forth.

Sam glanced at Esmeralda and there was fire in her eyes.

"Tsk, tsk," Brighton mused. "You really should have thought things through." His expression turned serious. "I'm a reasonable man, as you know from our prior interactions. I have a simple request for you two: I'll give you time to say goodbye to your families, yada yada yada, but you have seven days to turn yourselves in to the police and return Esmeralda to me, or I will send Miss Carmen to each of you in pieces."

The video went black.

Chapter 6

Shatina was sick of Brighton Miller and the weight he had been holding over her and Max's heads. They had to take him down, once and for all.

Sam looked pissed. "Brighton sent that video the day I entered the psych ward, which means he had to know we wouldn't have seen it until at least today. What if they kept me longer? Carmen could be dead! We only have three more days to pull this off, guys!"

Shatina grabbed the phone from Sam's hands.

"What are you doing?" Sam asked, startled at Shatina's sudden movement during her rant.

"Bring me another burner," Shatina replied.

Sam calmed, then nodded as if she understood what Shatina was about to do and brought her another burner from the back room. Shatina went through the activation process for the phone while everyone watched. Then she sent a text to Brighton Miller.

We received your message but going forward you will contact us at this number. No more games.

"Are you going to turn yourself in?" Shatara asked.

Shatina studied her sister's expression but couldn't read it. Did Shatara understand what turning herself in would lead to? Did she want Shatina to face life in prison for something she didn't do? Of course, there was a lot that she did do, but she wasn't the one who murdered Rodney that night. Brighton was. She shot him, but it was only to save Max from being killed. "I don't know," she answered, hoping that would be enough to appease her sister for now.

"What do you mean you don't know?" Shatara said, at the same time Jared said, "You're actually considering it?"

Shatina blew out a breath. "Guys, I probably know less about how to handle this situation than you do. My goal is to get Carmen out of there. If turning myself in is what it takes, yes, I'm willing to do that. But at the same time, if I turn myself in, it could lead to trouble for more than just me."

Jared's expression hardened. "You would snitch?" He straightened up, a fierce expression on his face, but Shatina wasn't fazed.

"No, I'm not saying I would snitch. What I am saying is that the police aren't stupid. They're going to know that I wasn't working alone with what I did. That would likely lead to a deeper investigation into my life, and it wouldn't take a rocket scientist to trace me to Max, and probably Sam, and who knows what else they might find."

Jared nodded as if he understood, but Shatara was still seething.

"You really think you can get away with this," she said as if in disbelief.

"Like I told you, Shatara, you never truly get away with anything. I've made my mistakes and I wish I could turn back the hands of time, but I can't. I've done things that I will live with for the rest of my life, whether or not I end up in prison."

Shatara wasn't satisfied by that answer, Shatina could tell, but she didn't say anything else.

"Let me get that phone," Jared said, reaching for the burner from Brighton.

Shatina handed it to him, and he was about to throw it to the floor when it buzzed with a new message.

"What now?" Shatina asked, irritated that Brighton was bothering them again. He had already made his point. They got it. Turn themselves in, and send Esmeralda back, or Carmen dies.

Jared checked the message. "This one is from an actual number, not a private number." His brow creased in confusion.

"What does it say?" Shatina asked.

Jared read the words slowly. *"We're at a point where we both need a friend. I'll help you if you help me."*

"Who could that be?" Sam asked.

"It's a trick!" Rambo quipped.

"Ask them who they are," Shatina said. "Tell them to reveal themselves if they're serious."

Jared typed the message and less than a minute later, a picture message was received.

"Tony," he said with his lip curled in disgust.

"Who's Tony?" Sam and Shatara asked in unison.

"He's Brighton's right hand since Ate got murked by Esmeralda."

Shatina looked at Esmeralda, but she turned her head in embarrassment. "No need to feel bad," Shatina said. "I appreciate you for helping us get out of there and for helping me get my sister back."

Esmeralda looked at the ground first, then raised her head to face Shatina with tears in her eyes. She nodded.

Something dawned on Shatina. "Seth mentioned that Tony had been helping him too. He said Tony gave him the info on Shatara, and he used that to help us. Remember?" She could feel herself getting excited. Maybe there was a way out of this after all.

Jared and Rambo didn't look convinced.

"Give me his number," Buster said from his wheelchair. He had to take it easy with his injuries, but Buster had agreed to help the crew with this final mission in any way he could.

Shatina read the number out loud and Buster saved it to his phone.

"I'll let you know what I find on him," Buster said. "For now, you should give him the number to the new burner and tell him we'll be in touch."

"What? No!" Jared said. "Tony is a high ranking member of Blue Street. There's no way we can trust this guy!"

***

The crew faced a huge dilemma. Jared, Slim, Luke, and Rambo believed Tony couldn't be trusted because of his status in Blue Street, while Max, Shatina, Sam, and Buster wanted to give him a chance. Shatara didn't know what to think, and Esmeralda remained silent.

Max turned to Esmeralda. "Do you think Tony can be trusted? Did you have any interactions with him?"

Esmeralda blinked back tears. "I don't know. Most of the time I had to deal with Ate and Brighton."

From the way she said that, Max recognized that Esmeralda had likely endured much trauma at the hands of those evil men. Who knew what this woman had gone through? They had to get Carmen back.

"I don't think this is a good idea, bro," Jared said.

"What other options do we have?" Max said. "Do you have any other connections into the Blue Street gang or into Brighton Miller?"

Jared didn't answer, which let Max know he didn't.

Max watched along with the rest of the crew as Jared took the burner outside the front door of the cabin, smashed and stomped it with his boot, then picked up the pieces to throw in the nearby pond.

When he returned, Rambo was in the middle of taking his side.

"Like I said, I think Jared's right," Rambo was saying. "Yes, Tony helped Seth, but Seth was also down with Blue Street. Just because he helped his boy doesn't mean he will help us, especially if he knows that you and Jared are brothers."

Max thought about it. Rambo did have a point. "But why would he go through the trouble to reach out to us then? Do you really think it's a trick or could Tony be sincere?"

Buster spoke up again. "Let me gather some intel about this guy to see if I can find anything. How about we go from there?"

That seemed to be a good idea, so the crew agreed to let Buster work his magic.

***

Tony and Carmen relished in the few moments they had together. Flex and Brighton were upstairs in the club, and Tony was supposed to be doing rounds throughout the basement to check on all the girls.

Instead, he spent his time in a liplock with the love of his life.

When they pulled back, Carmen's lips were swollen from the kiss.

"Hey," he said softly. "I might have some good news."

Her eyes lit up. "What is it?"

Tony spoke slowly, praying internally that his plan would work. "I might have a connection to get you out of here."

Her eyes filled with tears. "Are you sure?"

Tony nodded. "Yes, I'm sure."

But he wasn't sure. He was moving off hope and a prayer that Shatina and Max wouldn't cross him. Part of him was sure they wouldn't since they had saved Esmeralda. Why not her sister?

He couldn't let Carmen know the full extent of his thoughts, but he hoped like hell he was right.

A text came through on Tony's phone from Brighton. *Are you done?*

He had to finish his round.

"I'll see you later baby," he said, then kissed her one more time.

She nodded, but sadness filled her features and Tony wished more than ever that he could make it better.

This plan had to work.

Tony completed the rest of his round and as he climbed the stairs to meet Flex and Brighton in the club, his mind went to Seth.

Convincing Seth to join Blue Street was the biggest mistake of Tony's life. He should have known Seth wasn't cut out for the gang. Seth was no gangster, he was a good boy, running a basketball camp for Christ's sake.

Tony wasn't thinking. All he saw was a way to make more money.

Now one of his oldest friends was dead.

Chapter 7

The crew decided that splitting up would be the most effective way to handle things. Sam and Buster needed time to heal, so they were going to Sam's house.

"I'll go with you guys!" Shatara announced, and Sam shot her a weird look.

"Don't you want to stay with your sister?"

Shatina was staring at Shatara too, but Shatara refused to look in her direction. "Nope, I'm good. Plus I can help take care of Buster."

Buster blushed when she mentioned that, and Shatara's heart swelled. She wanted to be around him. They hadn't had a chance to talk much with the entire crew usually being in the room, but if there were only three of them at Sam's house, Sam would mostly be off to herself right? She seemed like a loner.

Sam gave Buster a look. "What do you think?"

Shatara didn't appreciate the understanding those two seemed to have. Had Buster and Sam dated? It was something about their shared glances at times that made Shatara suspect this. The tender way Buster spoke to Sam too. Maybe she was reading too much into it, but either way, Shatara was not staying with Shatina any longer.

"I don't mind," Buster said, and that settled it.

Shatara turned to Esmeralda. "Are you coming with us too?"

To Shatara's surprise, Esmeralda shook her head. "No, I want to be where the action is. I have to see my sister walk out of that place."

Shatara nodded. "Understood." She looked at the rest of the crew, careful not to glance in Shatina's direction. "What about you guys?"

Luke spoke up. "Whoever wants to stay with me, I don't mind."

"I'll stay with you," Jared and Rambo said in unison.

There was something about Jared and Rambo Shatara didn't like. They had helped tremendously in saving her from Brighton, and for that she was grateful, but apart from that, Jared and Rambo seemed too reckless. Besides, if they were in the middle of a gang war, Shatara wanted no part of that.

"I'll be around," Slim said, grabbing his coat. "Holler if you need me." That was a surprise. Shatara figured Slim would stay with Jared and Rambo since he was a gangster too. She watched as he dapped the rest of the guys up and walked out of Luke's house.

"You ready, babe?" Max shot Shatara a look like he was disgusted, then turned to Shatina. *What was that all about?*

Shatara didn't like Max either, so whatever. As far as she knew, him and Shatina were made for each other. They both were criminals.

After Shatina and Max left, Sam stood and walked over to grab Buster's wheelchair for him to sit in it. Shatara wished she had thought of that first, but her eyes were back on Esmeralda. "You're comfortable staying here with all guys?" she asked.

Esmeralda shrugged. "I don't mind."

"She's good," Luke said, and Shatara could have sworn she saw a hint of a smile on his lips. Okay, I see what's going on here.

Shatara didn't comment on it, but she was glad Esmeralda was finding some kind of enjoyment in this disastrous situation.

***

Sam wasn't sure how she felt about Shatara staying with her. Not that she had anything against the woman, but she wasn't about to sit there and listen to her talk about Shatina all day either.

She got that Shatara was pissed over almost being made a sex slave, but she was safe now. Get over it.

Maybe Sam was being harsh. Shatara had been thrown into a situation she knew nothing about, and from what Sam remembered of Shatina's diary, Shatina had done her sister dirty before. At the same time, Shatara had done her own dirt by sleeping with Shatina's man back in high school.

Sam wasn't getting in the middle of that. She had her own problems.

Like the fact that Robert still hadn't reached out to her. Did this mean he was over her? If so, that hurt. Did he know she tried to harm herself? Sam knew he wasn't aware of the baby. A thought dawned on Sam, stopping her in her tracks after she clicked her key fob to unlock her car doors. She had an appointment with her doctor for her first official ultrasound tomorrow. Robert deserved to know about it and Sam wanted him to be there, even if they weren't going to be together. Her eyes blurred with tears.

"Are you okay?" Shatara asked. She had taken over Buster's wheelchair and was pushing him to the car. "Do you need me to drive?"

Sam snapped out of it. "No, I'm good."

It was at that moment Sam remembered no one knew she was pregnant. What would they think of her if she made that announcement? They would probably be disgusted.

No time to focus on that.

Buster stood and got into the back seat and Sam and Shatara folded the wheelchair and put it in the trunk, then got into the driver's and front passenger's seats, respectively.

Sam had a lot to think about over the next few days, outside of Brighton Miller's looming threats.

***

Buster never thought he would be in this position. A gunshot wound to the chest at twenty one years old.

He was glad he survived, but still. This was going to take a lot of getting used to. At least he had a beautiful woman by his side to help him make it.

He smiled at that thought. Buster caught the vibes Shatara was giving off, and he threw her a few of his own.

He almost wished he could have Shatara come to his spot to take care of him, but he didn't want to leave Sam alone.

Buster worried about Sam, and he had felt that way for a while. None of the rest of the crew knew much about her, outside of maybe Max, but Buster felt like he knew Sam best.

He had known she was suicidal but wasn't sure how to approach her about it. He would have had to admit he had been snooping on her and watching her search history on her phone and laptop. Originally, he had done it for fun just to see what she was up to, but once he saw repeated searches on *how to kill yourself without pain*, it started to hit him. Sam dealt with a lot of issues, and from what Buster understood, she had no friends.

She barely talked to her mom, her relationship with her father was estranged, her ex-best-friend stabbed her in the back, her and Robert broke up, and she was only associated with Max and Shatina through blackmail before they reached the point of friendship.

Sam was a complex woman, but Buster knew that despite all her flaws, she had a good heart. She just needed love like everybody else. Buster hoped things worked out with her and Robert.

Maybe he could help?

Nah, he shook his head, deciding against it. His intervention in their relationship would only make things weird, especially if he revealed to Robert that he and Sam had been sleeping together before they linked up.

They pulled up to Sam's house and the women went to the trunk to get the wheelchair, but Buster protested.

"I'll walk into the house."

Shatara looked worried. "Are you sure?"

He nodded. "Luke said I needed to walk a few times a day, along with my breathing exercises. Gotta get my strength back."

Sam closed the trunk and they made their way to the front door.

Buster loved how Shatara felt walking next to him. She was about a head shorter than him and that turned him on. Something about having a woman look up into his eyes, and him looking down into theirs...

He hoped Sam stayed in her bedroom for the day.

51

Chapter 8

Tony seems clean, Buster had texted.

Max and Shatina's phones buzzed at the same time with the message. The whole crew had burner phones and were connected in a group text. Max and Shatina held the main burner that linked them to Tony and Brighton, while the others had regular burner phones.

Buster's message continued. *I was able to hack into his phone and from the looks of it, him and Carmen are in a relationship.*

Two photo messages came in after that. One was a selfie of Tony and Carmen in the basement of Brighton's club, and the other one was a screenshot of a poem he had written to her.

Shatina wrinkled her nose. "Tony and Carmen are in a relationship? Wow." There were surprises at every turn these days. Shatina wondered how Esmeralda felt about this news, then her mind traveled to her own sister. She couldn't say she was utterly shocked that Shatara had chosen to stay with Sam and Buster, but she didn't disagree that it was for the best. As hard as Shatina fought to get her sister away from Brighton, Shatara had brought nothing but stress to her life since they'd been reunited.

Shatina needed a break.

A text from Jared chimed into the chat. *Why doesn't he bust her out of there then?*

Max responded. *Don't be a tool, Jared. You know that's easier said than done.*

I still say we can't trust this guy.

We barely trust you!

Ouch.

Sam cut in. *We need a concrete plan. Time's ticking.*

How are things at your place? Rambo asked with a wink emoji. *Any room left for me?*

Jared sent laugh emoji's after that, but Sam didn't respond.

Shatina attempted to re-focus the crew. *I'm about to text Tony. Sam's right. Time is running out.*

Good idea, Max texted, and Shatina shot him a smile. She was lying on her couch with her feet in Max's lap. He smiled back at her and was about to say something when the phone buzzed again.

Please send us screenshots of all interactions, Buster texted. *Just so we're all in the loop.*

I'll do one better, Shatina texted. She created a new group text with the whole crew plus Tony. When her finger got to Shatara's name, she almost left her sister out of the text but decided not to be petty.

We're ready to talk, Shatina texted.

Tony wrote back almost immediately. *I'll reach out in a few. With the Boss.*

Shatina put her phone down on her end table, then watched as Max did the same. Now she was slightly worried.

"What's wrong?" Max asked.

"Do you think it was a bad idea to put everyone in the group chat with Tony?" By *everyone,* she meant Jared and Rambo, but she figured Max would catch her drift.

Max shrugged. "I wouldn't worry about it. Jared is reckless, but I don't think he would do anything to mess this up."

They stared at each other for a few moments, then Max shifted so Shatina's feet were no longer on his lap.

"Where are you...? Shatina started, then Max answered her question by climbing on top of her.

She wrapped her arms around his neck while he caressed her thighs.

"I couldn't wait to be alone with you," he said.

Shatina smiled, though her nose tinged. He always knew how to say the right things.

"Thank you for defending me earlier."

"Always." He lowered his lips onto hers.

As the kiss deepened, it became more erotic. Max's tongue entered her mouth, and Shatina felt herself begin to warm up.

She ran her hands up and down his back, then her fingers through his waves.

Max's hands were exploring her body as well.

Their phones buzzed with another text message, probably from one of the group chats, but neither of them moved to check it. This was their time, and no one was taking it from them. Max stood and removed his shirt, and Shatina scrambled off the couch to do the same. He had no idea how much she wanted him again since the first time they had been together like this.

The fire in his eyes let her know he had been feeling the same.

Shatina was about to lead him to her bedroom, but Max plopped onto the couch, his pulsing member in his hands. "Come sit with me," he said in a seductive tone.

Shatina caught the drift of what he truly meant.

She hadn't had much experience in this position because Seth was usually on top when they made love in the past, but she felt comfortable with Max. She only hoped she didn't hurt him.

She walked over and slowly lowered herself on top of him, straddling him, and he slid himself into her opening. It felt magical, but Shatina was still worried she didn't know what she was doing.

"Just do what feels good," Max murmured, and Shatina didn't need any further encouragement.

She began slow, careful rocking motions, but when Max's eyes rolled back, she was fully turned on.

Pretty soon they both were moaning each other's names and Max was gripping her thighs, thrusting himself into her from below.

Shatina let out a scream as she climaxed, and Max grunted his release shortly after.

Exhausted from the day's events, Shatina was ready to call it a night. A few moments later, Max stood with her still on top of him, carrying her to the bedroom.

Apparently, he was far from done.

***

Sam, Buster, and Shatara sat in the living room, watching a movie and waiting for Shatina or Max to respond to Tony's message.

I think I have a plan, he had texted.

Sam started getting antsy, so she responded before Jared or Rambo got any ideas. *What is it?*

Who's this?

You're in a group chat. No need for names to be exchanged.

Okay… I'll have to check back in later tonight. Boss just texted me.

Sam didn't know how to feel about that. She went to the other group chat to say something, then decided against it. She didn't want anyone accidentally sending a message to the wrong group. Instead, she turned to Buster and Shatara, who were watching their phones too.

"What do you think?" Sam asked. "He might be playing us."

Buster shook his head. "I wouldn't say that. I think he's really going to help but he's probably paranoid. Think about it. He's likely working alone from the inside since he mentioned needing a friend. If Brighton's over his shoulder, he has limited time to talk to us."

"Well he needs to hurry up and do so!" Shatara piped up. "Didn't Brighton say we only had three days left?"

Sam fought the urge to roll her eyes. As if Shatara was going to do anything useful to help this mission.

Then she stopped herself as she realized the reason she had such hostile thoughts toward Shatara was out of loyalty for Shatina. Sam let out a chuckle. *Wow. You never know how life is going to turn out.*

"What's funny?" Shatara asked.

"Nothing." Sam shook her head.

Buster looked like he wanted to know too, but Sam's regular phone began ringing with a call from her mom.

"Guys, I need to take this," she said, rising from her seat and heading toward her bedroom.

"Yes, Mom?" she answered.

"Honey, are you sure you don't want me to come over? I just need to see you."

Sam's mind went to Shatara and Buster in her living room. No way was she explaining their presence. "No Mom, I'm fine."

"Just for a few minutes. I'm on my way."

"Mom…"

She hung up.

Sam swore under her breath. She didn't want to do this right now.

Less than a minute later, a knock sounded at her front door. "Seriously?"

Sam had barely had time to think. She stomped toward the door, Buster and Shatara calling behind her to ask who was there.

She whipped it open, ready to send her away immediately. "Mom, I…"

Sam's breath caught in her throat as she dropped her phone.

It wasn't her mom standing on the other side of the door. It was Robert.

"You came," she let out, then became overcome with emotion. Her face reddened as floodgates of tears threatened to be released through her long lashes.

Robert looked like he was choked up too, but he blinked it back. "How are you?" he asked in a low voice.

"Come in," Sam gestured, completely forgetting she had guests.

Robert walked in and did a double take when he saw Shatara and Buster.

Sam snapped out of it. "Sorry. I… I wasn't thinking. This is Shatara, Shatina's sister and my friend, Buster."

Robert nodded at them in greeting but looked like he now felt awkward.

"You look familiar," Shatara said as she squinted.

"He's Max's dad. We're dating. *Were* dating," she corrected, before Robert could embarrass her.

Shatara's eyes widened at this news. "Oh... okay."

Sam turned back to Robert. "Do you want to talk in my room?"

Robert opened his mouth to answer, but Sam saw movement outside. She still hadn't closed the door behind him, and now her mother was striding up to her front porch with a cardboard box full of items.

"Oh!" Her mother's eyes widened with surprise when she saw Robert. "I didn't realize you had company."

"That's what I was trying to tell you," Sam answered. "I have a few friends over."

Her mother looked relieved. "Okay, I just wanted to make sure you were good and bring you a few things. We'll chat later."

Sam watched as Robert took the box from her mother.

"And who are you, young man?" her mother eyed him, seeming to sense the connection between her daughter and the mysterious gentleman she had never met.

"He's my boyfriend. Thank you for the care package, Mom."

Her mother caught the drift. "Okay, well nice meeting you, young man."

"Nice meeting you too, Ma'am," Robert said, then they watched as her mother left. Sam closed the door and Robert carried the box into her kitchen.

There were all kinds of goodies inside, plus a few items Sam knew her mother packed to make her feel better. Sam's favorite snacks, a new bathrobe and slippers, a massager, a self care journal, some candles, and a romance novel.

Sam didn't know if it was the hormones or what, but she found herself fanning her face to hold back her emotions.

She and her mother were always close, though Sam hadn't told her the half of what she'd been up to lately. Still, her mother put such care into this gift box. Sam had half a mind to call her back and give her a hug.

She focused back on Robert.

"I should go," he said, looking uneasy.

"No! You just got here. We need to talk."

"I didn't realize you had guests."

"We can talk in my room. Seriously."

He turned to leave. "No, I don't think that's a good idea."

Why was he acting like this?

Robert walked back toward the door, but Sam couldn't let him leave. She was about to make a fool of herself, but she darted around him and blocked the front door.

"Robert, we need to talk. I'm pregnant."

Stunned silence filled the room.

***

Tony and Flex were doing their late afternoon round to check on the girls. There were twenty girls in all, each housed in their own individual rooms in the basement. Brighton was so arrogant he didn't have locks on their

59

doors, and the girls were so afraid that none of them dared try to escape, except Shatara.

None of them had the help she had though.

Tony hoped that Max and Shatina and whoever else they were down with would be willing to go through with his plan.

He couldn't seem to get a moment alone throughout the day though. They had eight rounds each day: two in the morning, four in the afternoon and early evening, and two later in the evening.

After that, Brighton locked the upstairs door that led to the basement from the outside. It was made of iron so there was no way out without a key.

Tony had risked his life doing so, but one night he snuck and stole the key while Ate was doing the final round of the night. He had a guy he knew who could make keys of any kind for a hefty price.

The guy met him in the parking lot of the club, and Tony kept watch while he used a portable machine to make a copy of the key in his car.

Tony had planned to release all the girls and disappear, but before he could, Max, Shatina, and their crew had busted Shatara and Esmeralda out and chaos ensued.

Now Brighton had tighter security surrounding the girls.

The club was supposed to be shut down after the shootings, but Brighton planned to still sneak and hold private auctions to sell girls. To ensure his undercover business ran smoothly and stay on the lookout for the police, Brighton had a bunch of guys from Blue Street working for him. Some did rounds in the hallway that led to the basement, and some stood by the front and back doors of the club.

It was a risky mission, and Tony would likely have to put a few of his own guys down to fulfill it, but for Carmen, he was ready to give his life.

Chapter 9

When Robert and Sam went to Sam's bedroom, Shatara could not wait to talk to Buster. "Did you know she was pregnant?" she whispered.

Buster shook his head. "That's a crazy position to be in too, especially now."

"Tell me about it."

They stared at each other for a moment. Shatara didn't want to pry into Sam's business, but she felt out of the loop with this group. Everyone else seemed to know each other, and she was just thrust in the middle. Buster seemed cool and friendly, while Sam was a little standoffish. That was understandable, considering what she had just been through on top of the fact that she was pregnant but still, Shatara felt out of place.

A voice in the back of her mind wondered if she shouldn't have just stayed with Shatina and Max after all. She was pissed at her sister, but at least she knew her…

"What are you thinking about?" Buster asked, staring at her.

Shatara blushed when she caught his gaze. Buster was unbelievably sexy. Those full, juicy lips were sitting there as if they were waiting to be kissed. Shatara wondered if Buster had a girlfriend? He hadn't mentioned anyone. Everyone else was all boo'd up. Why not give it a whirl?

"Are you seeing anyone?" Shatara asked.

Buster looked taken aback by her question. "Whoa," he chuckled. "Where did that come from?"

Now Shatara's ears were burning. She had jumped the gun. "Never mind, I was just making small talk..."

He cut her off. "No, I'm not seeing anyone."

Silence fell between them.

Shatara wondered if she should say something more, but Buster beat her to it.

"Want to get to know each other?"

She relaxed with a smile, glad he was feeling her too. She thought he was, but his responses threw her for a loop. "That sounds good to me."

***

Sam knew it was probably inappropriate to blurt something like that out in front of everyone, but she didn't want Robert to leave. If she had let him, who knew how long it would take for him to come back, if ever? It wasn't like they were together anymore. Robert didn't owe her anything, and part of her didn't blame him.

In his eyes, she cheated, and technically, she did, even if it was for a good cause.

Sam felt sick to her stomach. She hated the fact that she slept with Brighton, especially after he revealed that he had been playing her all along.

When they were safely behind her bedroom door, Sam apologized. "Look, I'm sorry for the way that just went down. I was..."

Robert held his hand up to stop her. "It's fine. I knew anyway."

Her jaw dropped. "You did?"

He nodded. "I was the one who found you, Sam. I saw the pregnancy test next to you. Did you do this because of me?"

He looked like it pained him to say the words, but Sam was stuck on the fact that he said he knew she was pregnant.

"If you knew I was pregnant, why didn't you reach out to me sooner? Do you not care? Did I really mean that little to you, Robert?" Her eyes pooled.

"No, not at all. Sam, I'm still in love with you. You know that. There's no way I could be over you that quick, regardless of what happened. I just needed time to process it, that's all."

Sam crossed her arms, not convinced. "Okay, but you were about to walk out the door without saying anything just now."

He looked down. "I know, but that was only because I didn't want to have this conversation in front of people."

"What conversation?" Sam grew paranoid all of a sudden. What was Robert saying? Did he not want the baby?

"Our situation is complicated, Sam. We just broke up."

"I know, but we were together when we laid down to make this baby. I'm keeping it, just so you know."

Robert looked offended by her remark. "Okay... nobody said you shouldn't keep it. I wouldn't want it any other way."

"So what are you saying? Do you want to try to make it work between us?"

"Let's not get too far ahead of ourselves."

"What are you saying then, Robert?" Sam tried to take the impatience out of her tone, but it was hard. Robert had no idea the effect he had on her heart.

"Listen, you cheated on me! Remember that? If I say I need time, I need time, okay?" Robert's voice raised slightly as if he were getting frustrated.

Sam took a step back, calming herself. "I'm sorry. I didn't mean to push you. It's just... I'm scared." Her face fell.

Robert slowly lifted her chin. "There's no reason to be afraid. We'll find a way to figure this out."

Sam wanted to ask more questions, but didn't want to push him. Instead, she said, "I have an appointment tomorrow for an ultrasound. I'm not sure how you..."

Her voice trailed off as he reassured her. "I'll be there."

***

Luke and Esmeralda were in Luke's bedroom, while Jared and Rambo were on the couch playing video games.

"What do you think they're doing in there?" Rambo asked after they had been gone a while. He held a smirk on his face.

Jared smirked back. "It doesn't take a rocket scientist." He shrugged. "I don't blame Luke. He needed to blow off some steam."

"Yo, that shootout was sick, right?" Rambo said.

Jared's smile faltered. He enjoyed the shootout as much as Rambo did, but there was a moment where things almost went bad.

"What?" Rambo said, noticing the change in Jared's expression.

Just then, they heard banging on the door.

"Open up! Come on, man!"

Jared and Rambo jumped up, guns drawn from their waists and ready for action as they approached the door.

Luke scrambled out of the bedroom, shirtless while carrying a shotgun. Esmeralda was peeking around the corner.

The banging continued.

"Is that Slim?" Rambo asked.

Jared thought he recognized the voice too. He peeked through the blinds, then put his gun down and opened the door.

Slim practically collapsed inside, drenched in sweat. "Close the door!"

Jared obeyed. "What the hell happened man."

Slim panted, trying to catch his breath. "They tried to kill me!"

"Who?" Jared and Rambo said in unison.

Slim gulped more air, his heavy breathing beginning to subside. "Blue Street. Kato and them. I ran all the way from 6th Ave."

Jared and Rambo shared a look. 6th Ave was several blocks away.

"Did anyone see you come here?" Luke asked.

Slim shook his head. "No. They caught me outside the corner store. I wasn't close enough to my car so I had to gun it. They shot at me and I shot back, but ran out of bullets. I lost them after I hopped a few fences, but I didn't have anything else on me so I came here."

"Damn," Jared said. "So your car is still parked outside the store?"

Slim nodded.

"Let's go get it," Rambo said, looking pissed.

Jared stopped him. "Not right now. Let's wait til later tonight and get it then."

"Why not now?" Rambo looked perplexed.

"We have too many things going on. We'll get his car back, relax, but for now we need to lay low."

Rambo looked like he still wanted to go but backed down. "A'ight bet."

Chapter 10

The crew received several voice clips from Tony shortly after midnight. His plan was simple and straightforward, but deadly.

Max turned to Shatina. "What do you think?"

She sighed. "I think I want this to be over."

Max was shocked at that response, but he felt the same. "Me too. It's almost over though."

"Is it?" A tear appeared in the corner of her eye. "Is it ever over, Max? Every time we think it is, here comes more trouble. We're out of the frying pan and into the fire. We never get a break."

Now she was scaring him. "Don't think like that. We have to keep hope."

"For what though? What do we have to hope for? We keep getting thrust into these situations and scraping by through the skin of our teeth, but then what? Where do we go from here? My sister hates me, and if my parents ever find out what I've done I'm sure they will disown me too."

Max paused. He thought of his own parents. They hadn't disowned him per se, but they discarded him long ago, which almost felt worse than being disowned. Once

Jared came around, he was seen as the Golden Child, while Max was a throwaway.

Shatina continued. "Seth is dead. I can't stop thinking about it. It was my fault."

Her voice broke.

Max wrapped his arms around her. "No, I'm not going to let you do that to yourself."

"He came back trying to help me."

"But his involvement was his own choice. You can't blame yourself for his decisions. He told us he was out there running with Blue Street. I appreciate what he did by helping us, but he did bring it on himself. You didn't even know he was coming back, Shatina, and remember, you left him at Disney World. You chose to come back because you were trying to face your issues and not run from them. Nobody could have foreseen this."

Max stared at Shatina as he spoke and it looked like his words were going in one ear and out the other. That hurt, but he hoped something stuck.

"We'll be okay," he finished.

She didn't respond.

***

Shatina and Max pulled up to Sam's house to talk about Tony's plan. Shatina appreciated Max for trying to comfort her, but she felt like she was at her wits end.

Her mind and body were fatigued.

She wanted out.

"You good?" Max asked after they had been sitting outside of Sam's house for over five minutes.

"Yeah," Shatina replied and got out of the driver's seat. At first, she looked over her shoulder to make sure no one was following them. Jared had called and told Max that someone shot at Slim.

As if they didn't already have enough problems.

He kept reassuring them that Blue Street was after them, and not the rest of the crew, but Shatina had learned that you couldn't be sure of anything these days.

It was best that they watched their backs, but again, what for?

Maybe they were better off just turning themselves in to the police, like Shatara kept suggesting.

Shatina flirted with the idea as Max knocked on the front door.

She stared at his profile.

No, Max wouldn't want to do that. He would want to fight this through, take their chances, and hope to come out on the winning side.

Even if they won, would the battle be over? Judging from everything that happened so far, the answer was probably no.

Sam opened the door.

Buster and Shatara were also awake, which was strange considering that it was almost one o'clock in the morning, but Shatina figured they were getting just as much rest as she was lately, which was none.

Shatina looked at her sister. Shatara was still avoiding her eyes, which half infuriated her, and the other half was in pain.

Pain seemed to be her go-to emotion these days.

She shrugged it off, or at least tried to.

"What do you guys think of the plan?" Max asked when everyone was settled.

Sam sighed. "To be honest, it worries me."

That perked Shatina up. Sam didn't want to do it either? Shatina studied her expression. Sam had changed since they first met. She was a certified bad girl, living on the edge, wild and carefree. Since she'd been involved in the situation with Shatina and Max, Sam had slowly lost herself, to the point where she tried suicide.

This wasn't good.

They had to end this.

They couldn't keep doing this to themselves.

Shatina studied Shatara next, who was still avoiding her. She sucked her teeth, but no one seemed to notice because they were engrossed in the conversation about the plan. Shatara was in many ways similar to Sam before all this. She wasn't the type to start trouble with people, but her sister was as carefree as they came. Now she was trapped into a situation she had nothing to do with. That part was Shatina's fault, regardless of what Max said. He could only comfort her so much before he had to admit that a large part of her problems, Shatina brought on herself.

To a degree, they all did.

This was a mess.

Something had to give.

"I don't know," Sam was saying in response to whatever Buster just said. Shatina hadn't been paying attention. Sam continued. "It's like, we don't know Tony, me and Buster are injured, and Jared and Rambo are embroiled in a gang war. There are too many factors against us."

"There always have been," Max countered. "I hear you Sam, but we don't have a choice. Even if we don't try to save Carmen, Brighton won't stop coming after us."

That seemed to settle it for Buster and Sam, Shatina could tell. They were reluctant but agreed. Shatina no longer knew where she stood on the matter.

***

Sam was nervous as all get-out when it was time to go to the ultrasound appointment. Robert said he was coming to pick her up, but did that mean he was open to them rekindling their relationship?

Sam didn't want to get too far ahead of herself, as Robert suggested, but she needed answers. She would never have chosen to be a single mother, especially under the circumstances she was under, but if that was her lot in life, she was willing to accept it.

The baby had given her a second chance at life. A new direction to go. A clearer mindset. Or at least Sam hoped so.

Who was she kidding?

She didn't know the first thing about being a mom.

Sam didn't have a job. Dexter was paying all her bills.

She had flirted with the idea of opening her own salon in the past, but even that was a silly fantasy where she wouldn't actually do any work, just have other people run it while she collected money.

Sam needed to get a grip.

Part of her was excited, while the other part was trembling in fear.

Robert showed up.

"Hey," he said in a soft voice, but Sam couldn't read his expression. She decided not to agonize over it.

Go with the flow.

They didn't talk much on the way to the doctor's office, and when they saw the receptionist, Robert kept a lighthearted tone.

What was his angle?

Sam was trying not to, but it was hard not to wonder what he was thinking.

Her mind finally refocused when the tech spread the jelly on her belly. Sam giggled as she imagined those words playing over a trap beat. *Jelly on my belly, ayyee!*

Robert smiled too.

Her heart warmed.

When they saw the image, the tiny bean looking thing on the screen, Sam melted. This was real. A living, breathing being was going to come from her body.

Her throat constricted as her mind filled with awe.

"Wow," Robert said, and his word echoed her thoughts completely.

Chapter 11

When Sam left for her doctor's appointment, Shatara and Buster finally had some time to themselves.

He looked like he was zoned out for a second, then he turned to her.

"What?" she asked.

"This situation is wild."

"Agreed."

He studied her as if curious. "What are you thinking? Do you think we should go through with Tony's plan? I noticed you didn't say much when Max and Shatina came last night."

Shatara grew tongue-tied. Why was he asking her opinion? She gathered her bearings.

"If I had to be honest I would say everyone is going about this the wrong way."

Buster looked intrigued by that response, so she continued.

"As much as nobody wants to say it, I think Max and Shatina should turn themselves in."

Buster looked like he was with her for a second, until he realized what she was saying.

"What?" he asked as if in shock. "Do you realize what could happen if she does that?"

Shatara didn't understand why he seemed so upset with her. "It's the right thing to do."

"There is no right in this situation, Shatara. Only a series of options and the hope you're choosing the best one."

Shatara didn't like his train of thought. "And *the best one* as you put it is for them to turn themselves in."

Buster turned his body more so he was directly facing her. "You really think Brighton's going to release Carmen if Max and Shatina turn themselves in? You're crazy if you do. Have you seen how that man operates? He was gonna sell you if we didn't save you, regardless of what Max and Shatina did. If they do what he said he wants, he's not going to do the right thing. If Esmeralda goes back to him, he'll probably torture her and her sister or worse. You have to think of other people outside of yourself."

Buster's words were hitting Shatara in ways she didn't like. From his tone she could tell he was trying not to be condescending, but she still felt like she was being spoken to like a child.

At the same time, she had to admit he had a point.

She was about to tell him so, but he turned the TV on, obviously still pissed at her perspective.

Why ask my opinion then, if you didn't want it? Shatara wanted to respond with attitude but left it alone instead.

***

Shatina tried her best to get rest after she and Max returned to her apartment, but she couldn't. He kept asking her if she was okay, but that only made things worse.

Finally, she laid still and breathed deeply to pretend that she was asleep. That seemed to work on Max. She heard him snoring less than an hour later.

But Shatina wasn't asleep. She couldn't rest until this was over.

***

Buster tried his best to look at situations from multiple angles and give everybody the benefit of doubt, but Shatara was starting to irk him.

Did she hold no compassion in her heart for her sister?

Shatina was doing what she could to navigate this situation just like everybody else. Why was Shatara set on seeing her fall?

Maybe Buster was being harsh.

He didn't think Shatara wanted Shatina to fall. She was probably just frustrated and this was her way of expressing that.

He relaxed. Soon, this situation would be over and they could go back to their normal lives. Buster had spent so much time worrying about everyone else he hadn't thought of himself.

What was he going to do with his future?

He was great with technology and had a promising career until his boss played him and got him fired. Now his name and reputation were tarnished. Even though the company didn't go public with the report about Buster supposedly stealing money from the grant, people still talked. Buster was better off going into business himself, but did he have what it took?

It was something to contemplate.

His mind traveled to what he had done to Max and Shatina. He glanced at Shatara, wondering what she would think of him if he told her about that.

Chapter 12

J ared and Rambo had crept out in the wee hours of the morning to get Slim's car. Slim was sleeping on Luke's couch, but Jared and Rambo hadn't been outside in a while so they decided to do him one solid.

Guns fully loaded, they rode to the corner store where Slim's car was parked. Miraculously, it was still there, but Slim was gonna be pissed when he saw his missing rims. The driver's side window was also broken, indicating they had probably stolen his stereo system too. Jared got out to investigate, Slim's key in one hand (not that he needed it, seeing that the window was broken) and his other hand on his Glock which was situated in his waistband. He opened the car door and swept glass off the driver's seat, simultaneously confirming his suspicions. The area where the stereo system was usually housed was completely empty with a wire hanging out of it.

"Ayo," he heard Rambo say, then a gun cocked nearby. A grin formed on Jared's face. Showtime.

He whipped out his own gun and turned around. Rambo was already doing the same and they both had guns pointed at them from some Blue Street guys. One was Kato, the guy Slim said shot at him, and the other was Six, a punk Jared never liked.

"Y'all must have really wanted to see us, huh?" Jared said. "You waited here all day?"

Kato wasn't interested in conversation. "Your boy was over here in our territory. His fault, not ours, plus we already have problems."

Jared knew exactly what Kato was referring to, as him and Rambo had robbed and killed quite a few Blue Street men. He shrugged. It was part of the game. Parker Square lost guys too.

"How are we gonna handle this?" Jared said in a tone that let Kato know he was down for whatever.

His mind flashed to Max. He was supposed to be helping his brother, and if he died tonight, that obviously wouldn't happen. That sobered him a little.

Kato cracked a smile. "I'm a reasonable man. I'll let you slide this once, but just know we're coming for you soon."

Jared chuckled. This guy was a joke. Had a whole gun in his hand and was afraid to pull the trigger.

"I gotchu," he responded and nodded at Rambo.

Kato and Six put their guns down and began backing away, their eyes still on Jared and Rambo. Rambo got in his car, while Jared entered Slim's.

He turned the key in the ignition and it worked. Thank God.

He eased away from the sidewalk, heading down the street behind Rambo when gunshots sounded from behind.

He sucked his teeth. Jared should have known those punks would wait til his back was turned. Rambo's car was leaning to the side, indicating one of his tires was out, and that pissed Jared to the max. He pointed his gun out the window and let off several shots of his own.

He heard yelling, which meant he must have hit one of them, so he increased his speed. Rambo did the same, though he only had three tires. They made it to the junkyard where one of their guys patched up Rambo's tire.

"I say we go back and get them," Rambo said, fire in his eyes.

Jared didn't appreciate the stunt Kato and Six pulled either, but now wasn't the time. "After the plan is over. I gotta help my brother."

Rambo was pissed but he backed down. "Once that's done it's on."

"You know it homie." They dapped each other up to seal the promise.

***

Shatina was done.

Since she couldn't sleep last night, she had plenty of time to think. It wasn't what she wanted, but she had to do something to make all this stop.

She wanted it to be over.

When Max went into the bathroom to take a shower, Shatina waited until she heard the water running and him sliding the curtain aside to step in.

She was going to miss him, miss everyone, but there was no other way out of this.

Leaving her cell phone and the burner phone on the kitchen counter, Shatina scrawled a quick note.

I'm sorry Max, she wrote. *Tell everyone I wish things were different, but I had to do something to get us out of this.*

After that, she stood in the kitchen, staring at the note til her eyes blurred, then hurried out the door before Max could realize she was gone.

***

Shatara couldn't take Buster's silence anymore. They were watching reruns of one of her favorite sitcoms, but neither of them were laughing. Buster looked like he was deep in thought, and Shatara wanted to pick his brain.

She opened her mouth to speak, but before she could get a word out, Max's number flashed on her screen.

She wrinkled her nose. "Why is Max calling me?"

That seemed to snap Buster out of his funk. "Answer!" he said.

Shatara pressed the green button. "Hello?"

"What did you say to her?" he boomed.

"What are you…"

"Shatina is gone!"

Shatara's body filled with shock. "What do you mean, she's gone?"

"She left her phone and the burner here and wrote a note basically saying she's turning herself in."

Shatara was taken aback. "She did?"

"What did you say to her, Shatara? Did you put her up to this? You've been gunning for her downfall since you got here."

"I have not…"

"Whatever, you just better hope I find her before she does something stupid!"

He hung up the phone.

Shatara hadn't realized she was crying until Buster handed her a tissue. "What just happened?" she asked. "I didn't say anything to her, I swear!"

81

Buster shook his head. "I don't know what's happening, Shatara. I just hope Max stops Shatina."

Shatara had half a mind to go after her sister herself, but the other part of her felt like she'd already ruined things enough.

Chapter 13

Sam's happy moment with Robert was deflated when she entered her house to find that Shatina had gone to turn herself in.

She dropped the bag of food she was holding when she heard the news. Robert had brought her to a drive thru and insisted he feed her since she was carrying his child.

He was being silly, she knew, but she suddenly had a taste for a burger when they pulled up.

Now that memory faded as the weight of Shatina's decision began to hit her. "Why did she do that?" Sam asked, thinking out loud more than anything else. She looked at Shatara.

"I didn't say anything to her, I swear!" Shatara said.

Buster walked over and picked up Sam's bag of food.

"Thanks," she said, then noticed the grimace on his face. "You okay?"

He nodded and breathed deeply. "I keep forgetting I have to be careful while I'm healing."

Sam studied the patch covering his chest beneath his wife beater. "You changed your bandage?"

He nodded. "Shatara helped me."

Sam caught his blush. She knew it. Those two had seemed like they were getting cozy lately. Good for them. Sam initially hadn't liked Shatara, then she decided to let her hostile feelings go, reasoning she had bigger things to worry about.

"Max went to find her," Shatara said, cutting back into the conversation.

Sam snapped out of it. "Right. I hope he finds her."

Shatara stared. "Are you okay?"

"Yeah, I'm good. I spaced out a second. Probably hormones or something." Sam went into the kitchen to eat her meal and think about Robert. She was worried about Shatina too, but she couldn't allow herself to dwell on it.

***

Max had circled the police station like a madman, but he didn't see Shatina's car parked outside. Had she changed her mind?

He waited over twenty minutes, but she didn't show up.

Then he went back to their apartment and she wasn't there either.

He drove by Sam's house and even Brighton's club but she wasn't in either of those places either.

There was one other possible place, but why would she go there?

Max's heart sank when he pulled up to Luke's spot and saw that Shatina wasn't there either.

His fists banged the steering wheel.

Where was she?

***

Shatina had initially headed toward the police station, then chickened out. When she left her apartment that morning, she felt her mind was clear.

She was turning herself in and it would solve all their problems.

Then the more rational side of her brain kicked in and reminded her that things weren't that simple.

Still, she desperately wanted this situation to be over.

She hit the highway, driving for about an hour until she reached a conclusion that felt right.

She breathed deeply every so often as she headed to her destination, hoping she made the right choice.

Shatina pulled up outside the police station, took another deep breath to ease her anxieties, then opened the car door.

Her legs felt wobbly, but this was what she had to do.

She would try her best to keep the rest of the crew out of this. She couldn't let any of them take the fall. This situation was on her, not them.

Her eyes blurred, but she blinked the tears back. It was time to put on her big girl panties.

Shatina had a fleeting thought of calling her mother, but shrugged that off too. No more stalling. Once she went to trial, her parents would find out what she had done. It would probably hit the news before sundown anyway.

She was barely three steps toward the building when a man turned the corner and walked into the parking lot, patting his pockets for his keys. He pulled them out, but Shatina wasn't focused on that. She was focused on the three huge letters stamped on the vest he was wearing, *FBI*, as well as the fact that this couldn't be real.

"Ted?" she said before she could stop herself.

Ted stopped short, just noticing her as he seemed to have tunnel vision toward his car.

Shatina stared from his vest, to his face, and back to his vest again. A flood of questions swirled in her mind. What the hell was going on here?

Ted seemed to notice her confusion. "I think we should talk."

Chapter 14

Flex and Tony started their late morning round, entering the basement through the iron door and thundering down the stairs. "You heard what happened last night?" Flex asked.

Tony shook his head. He wasn't interested in Flex's conversation, and he was even less interested in what could have happened last night.

Flex continued, not seeming to notice Tony's distraction. "Kato and Six got into it with those Parker Square guys, Jared and Rambo. Six got hit, but he made it."

"For real?" Tony mustered a response that he hoped resembled compassion for what was supposed to be one of his boys. He barely knew Six, but Tony was supposed to be loyal to the gang.

Flex nodded. "Jared's been a real problem ever since he got out. Everybody's eyes are on him, but he's sneaky. He keeps getting away. We gotta end him before he makes us look weak."

Tony grunted in response, but his mind was on Carmen. He had to get her out of here, get her away from Brighton Miller, and maybe start a new life with her somewhere else. If he got a few moments alone with her today, he was going to ask her where she would want to go.

"You good man?" Flex was eyeing Tony with suspicion.

Tony snapped out of it. "Yeah man, just a lot on my mind but I agree. We're gonna get him, no doubt. It's only a matter of time before he gets caught slipping."

Flex's face lit up at that. "Facts!" He and Tony dapped each other up, then parted ways to complete rounds on opposite sides of the long hallway.

***

Shatina had never been more shocked in her life. Ted was an FBI agent? Since when? She eyed him with suspicion as they sat across from each other at the coffee shop. It was a discreet location near the downtown area. Not many customers, and the staff were friendly. Shatina followed Ted there at his request, and he ditched his vest when he exited his vehicle.

Ted spoke first after they stared at each other for a few moments. "Shatina, what were you doing outside the police station?"

Her heart dropped. There was no way she could get around telling him something, since he saw her there clear as day. Still, she didn't know what information she could trust him with. He had lied about his identity after all. He owed her answers, not the other way around.

"You first," she countered. "Clearly you aren't who you've been saying you are. Since when have you been a cop? You worked at my school. Were you really a professor?" Shatina was confused as she tried to put the facts together. Ted had taught for the entire semester and she had earned a grade on her transcript. She even found as profile for him on *ratemyprofessor.com*! But how was he her professor if he was also a cop?

Ted swallowed. "Okay, I guess I owe you that. I'll talk first, then it's your turn."

***

Max's mind was going frantic. Shatina wasn't anywhere.

The cops didn't tow her vehicle, did they?

That was the only thing he could think of that had happened. But how could they get it done so quickly? Did she walk into the station, confess to Rodney's murder, then they threw her in a cell and took her car?

Max shook his head. That didn't make sense. Cops usually questioned you for hours. He knew that from his own experiences on the wrong side of the law.

Max refreshed his phone screen for the umpteenth time. Still no news updates.

Did Shatina ditch her car somewhere?

Why would she do that?

Max's breath caught in his throat as a more sinister thought emerged. What if Brighton got her? What if he had people watching them the whole time, and now Shatina was trapped in the basement of his club like those other girls?

If that was the case, Max was breaking in there. He would kill Brighton Miller with his bare hands if he had to.

Chapter 15

Brighton was sitting in his office enjoying a glass of Scotch. He loosened his tie and relaxed in his seat as McConnell had just told him the best news of his life.

He burst into his office, annoying him first because he didn't knock, but when Brighton saw the look on McConnell's face, he knew he had good news.

"Guess what?" he said.

"What?" Brighton braced himself, his lips already forming a smile.

"You were right. Shatina cracked first. She just went to the police."

"Hallelujah!" Brighton pounded his desk with elation. Once the police got their hands on Shatina, the wheels would turn in his favor. Their attention would undoubtedly turn to her and Max, and Brighton would be free to get back to his business.

He was losing money by not being able to host his sex parties at the club, but that didn't mean he stopped all activity.

Brighton's wicked grin widened. "This, my friend, is a cause for celebration."

McConnell already had his hands on the bottle of Scotch. "Indeed it is."

Brighton clapped his hands. "Oh, and guess what? We're doing a clean sweep tonight too. All the girls will be gone, then we'll lay low for a bit until we get a new crop."

McConnell nodded, and Brighton watched as he poured himself a glass, then gulped it down. Then McConnell turned back to Brighton, sporting a wicked grin of his own. "I guess you won't be releasing Miss Carmen then?"

They stared at each other for a few moments before they burst out laughing together. Brighton held his stomach. His abs were screaming, he hadn't laughed this hard in a long time.

"Did you sharpen my machete like I asked you to?" he asked McConnell when he caught his breath.

McConnell calmed himself. "I sure did. Are you getting rid of her tonight?"

Brighton shrugged. "I don't see why not. Make sure we record it too. I want Esmeralda to see and hear everything. Let her know what happens when you cross a man like me."

***

Vomit rose to the back of Tony's throat as he stepped away from Brighton's office door. This couldn't be happening.

When McConnell practically knocked him over trying to get inside the office, Tony was about to say something but stopped himself. His instincts told him that he needed to listen in on their conversation.

Now he didn't know what to do.

He walked aimlessly back down the hall, contemplating his options when Flex turned the corner and they bumped into each other.

"You good man? What's up with you?" Flex asked, looking concerned.

"I'm good," Tony assured. "Bout to go on a run real quick then I'll be right back."

Flex stared for a minute. "No doubt," he said, and they dapped each other up before Tony left.

When he got to his car, he fired off a series of texts to the chat.

Things changed. We have to move tonight. Plus, we have to get all the girls out, but I have a plan for that too.

He wasn't sure if the crew would agree to helping all the girls and not just Carmen, but his conscience would never forgive him if he didn't at least try.

No one wrote back, but Tony couldn't think about that right now. They had to help him. Time was running out.

***

Since no one answered the messages Tony sent, Jared took it upon himself to respond. He called Tony's number.

"Yo," Tony answered, sounding frantic.

Jared put him on speaker as Rambo, Luke, and Esmeralda listened in.

"What do you mean, we have to get all the girls? We were only supposed to grab Carmen. You know twenty girls at once is too risky!"

"We have to, man! He's planning to sell them all tonight. I can't have that on my conscience. This guy is sick!"

"It's still too risky."

"He's gonna kill Carmen! I heard him say it to his lawyer. I can't let her die, man." Tony's voice cracked as if he were at his wits end.

When Esmeralda heard Brighton's plans for Carmen she stood. "Tony, you have to get my sister out of there!" She snatched the phone out of Jared's hands.

"I need you guys to help me though. I'm only one man."

"We will," she reassured, then turned to Jared and the rest of the guys, her tone venomous as if threatening them to say they weren't down.

Jared held his hands up as if to say you got it, while Rambo looked conflicted. Luke nodded.

"Okay," Tony said, his voice calming. "I'll text you with more details in a few."

***

Max's mind swam when he entered Luke's spot to tell them about Shatina and found out that not only had the plan been moved up to tonight, but that they now had agreed to help save all the girls, not just Carmen.

"You told him what?" Max said to Jared.

Before Jared could answer, a series of texts started coming to the chat. Tony sent the location and pictures of the guys who were guarding the black vans the girls had been thrown into the night of the shooting.

They're bulletproof, so we need them, he texted. *There are four vans total, but only three guys should be guarding the spot. Use silencers. Let me know when you get them and I'll work on things from inside the club. There can't be any witnesses or everything is ruined.*

Max was at a loss for words. They were about to make the biggest mistake of their lives if this plan fell through.

"We're down," Jared said, breaking into his thoughts.

"I'll be on standby if you guys need me," Luke said, offering his medical support.

They were officially backed against a wall. The only way out was to start swinging.

Chapter 16

Shatara had been on the edge of her seat ever since she heard that Shatina had gone missing. She texted Max privately, in case he hadn't told his brother and the rest of the group about Shatina going to the cops.

Any news?

No. But we got bigger fish to fry now.

Bigger fish to fry? What was Max...?

A knock sounded on Sam's door. She opened it, and Max walked in.

"Have you guys been receiving the texts from the chat?" he asked.

Sam spoke up. "Yes, but what is Tony talking about? We were waiting for you to respond since Shatina is gone."

Max looked pissed. "Apparently, Jared took things into his own hands and called Tony."

Shatara gasped. "He what?"

Max continued. "Jared told him we were down to do the plan tonight and try to save all the girls."

Buster blinked. "Wow. I don't think that's a good idea man."

"Me either, but that's where we are now. It's already in motion."

Shatara thought about her sister. Where she was and what she could be doing now. Had the police officially arrested her? Was she in the middle of giving them a statement? Time would only tell, but the more the day wore on, the guiltier Shatara felt.

***

Shatina listened as Ted launched into his explanation. "As you gathered, yes, I'm in the FBI. I have been for a number of years."

Her eyes narrowed. "So that story you told Max about going to jail and fighting your way through college..." Her voice trailed off as he held his hands up.

"Some of that was true. I was locked up around the time he was born and they did take my rights away. When I got out I tried to fight it but nobody wanted to help me. I got in more trouble, and when I faced the judge, he said I had the option to go to jail or the military. I chose the military."

Shatina was stunned as Ted continued, telling her that he rose up in ranks and when he was discharged, he was so well-respected that one of the lieutenants nudged him to try for the FBI. Since the lieutenant had connections, Ted was allowed in. He'd worked a number of assignments, but the Brighton Miller case was the biggest one of his career.

Shatina's jaw dropped. "You've been tracking Brighton Miller?"

Ted nodded. "I'm only telling you this because I know some of what's been going on with you, Shatina. I know you were involved in a recent murder that Brighton was charged with."

Shatina wasn't prepared for that one. "What? How do you..."

Ted continued. "I thought it was a coincidence at the time that you were connected to Max in high school, but when I saw you with him while I tailed him one day, I put two and two together that you had a deeper connection. Then the fact that you were connected to one of my informants, Seth. All the pieces started to point to you."

Shatina blinked back tears. "So this whole time you were investigating me? Do you even care about Max?"

"Of course I care about Max! He's my son. It's purely a coincidence that he happens to be involved in the case too."

Shatina wasn't convinced. "What about Sam? You told her you had no idea she was the girl Max was trying to kill. Was that a lie too?"

Ted didn't answer.

Shatina was disgusted. "You really are a piece of work."

She stood to leave, but Ted grabbed her arm to stop her.

"Sit back down. We had an agreement, remember? I need you to tell me everything you know and everything you've been involved in, if you want to have any chance of getting out of this."

Shatina was stuck. She had no choice but to continue this conversation, but she was still deeply confused. She sat back in her seat. "Why were you at my school?"

Ted sighed. "The professor job was a cover. I do have a few years of experience teaching different college courses, but your school was part of my assignment. The class was a way to communicate freely with Seth originally, and when he was shot the first time, I was about to give it up. Then I realized you were still taking the class and decided to stay."

"And that's why you targeted me throughout the semester," Shatina finished.

Ted didn't respond to that. Instead, he stared at her. "Your turn."

***

Brighton's guys didn't know what hit them.

Two of them were returning to the garage with bags of food while the other stood watch. Slim pulled up in slow motion while Jared, Rambo, and Esmeralda poked their heads out the car windows. Jared was in the front passenger's seat, while Rambo and Esmeralda were on the rear driver and passenger's sides, respectively.

Bullets flooded from their silenced guns, pelting the men's bodies with no mercy. They watched as all three of them went down, then they looked around for witnesses.

The garage was located at the end of a dead end street across from an abandoned building. Perfect location for shady dealings like the ones they were engaged in now.

The group moved quickly.

Jared found the keys in one of the fallen men's pockets. He opened the garage doors and the others tumbled into the vans, grabbing the keys to the vehicles from a holder on the garage's interior wall. They each backed their vans out, then drove Slim's car inside, putting the three bodies into the car. One across the driver's seat, one across the passenger's, and one in the trunk.

98

Esmeralda kicked dirt over some of the blood that was on the ground but there was no way to cover it all.

"That's the best we can do for now," Jared said, closing the garage doors with Slim's car and the bodies inside. "I hope Tony was right about these being the only three guys or your sister's probably a goner."

Chapter 17

It was Shatina's turn to speak but she wasn't sure what to say. "First of all, I didn't kill Rodney," she stated.

"I did shoot him, but only to save Max. He had a gun pointed at his head."

Ted's forehead was creased as he listened intently. "So you and Max showed up with a gun?"

She shook her head. "No. Me and Max suspected that Rodney killed Seth. He was my fiancé and I wanted revenge. Neither Max or I had a weapon, but Rodney had two guns." She went on to explain how the fight happened and how Max ended up with a gun to his face, forcing her to pull the trigger on Rodney.

"But he wasn't dead, I swear. He was still moving and me and Max saw Brighton kill him. We got the whole thing on video."

Ted nodded as the wheels appeared to turn. "You and Max sent the video to the police."

"Yes, but then Sam sent more footage and..." She shook her head. "Anyway, there are more pressing matters at hand. The reason I went to the police station today."

Ted was all ears. He leaned forward. "Talk to me."

Shatina tried to choose her words carefully. "Do you know anything about Brighton's other activities, outside of drugs?"

Ted slowly nodded, his eyebrows raising as if he was surprised to learn that she knew more. *So he has no idea about Brighton kidnapping Shatara then,* Shatina reasoned.

"I know of a few activities. Go on," Ted prodded.

Shatina didn't know how else to say it, so she let it out. "Brighton's involved in sex trafficking. He has at least twenty girls locked in the basement of his club, one of them being my friend's sister. That's why I came to the station."

Ted didn't look surprised anymore when Shatina revealed that Brighton was a sex trafficker. "Shatina," he started, then his cell phone rang.

Shatina tried to glance at the screen to see who was calling but Ted snatched the phone up before she could make out the name of the contact.

"Hello?" Ted answered.

A muffled voice sounded on the other line. Shatina couldn't make out what they were saying, but judging from the fact that Ted's demeanor darkened, she knew it wasn't good.

"Okay, got it," he said and ended the call. He blinked, then refocused on Shatina. "Come with me."

"Huh? We weren't finished…"

"Come with me. Now."

Shatina followed him out of the coffee shop, their drinks long forgotten.

***

We got the vans.

Buster, Shatara, and Sam sighed in collective relief. They were each sitting on pins and needles, afraid of all that could go wrong.

Now that they had the vans, it seemed the plan would work.

None of them felt prepared for this mission but it had to be done tonight if they had any chance of saving Carmen.

Chapter 18

Shatara was in the middle of celebrating the fact that they got the vans when her phone lit up with a call from Tyonne, her cousin.

She clapped her hand over her mouth.

Shatara had been so engrossed in this mission that she completely forgot about her cousin and her other best friend, Tamika.

She had meant to speak with them after being cursed out by her parents, but all the recent activity caused it to escape from her mind.

"Who's that?" Buster asked, glancing at her phone.

Shatara stood. "My cousin. I need to take this."

"Make sure you don't tell them anything about what's going on!" Buster called out as she entered the privacy of Sam's bathroom.

"Hello?" she answered.

Tyonne's voice was full of attitude. "Oh, so you just gonna disappear for over a week, refuse to answer anybody's phone calls or texts, then finally answer like nothing happened? Girl, what's wrong with you?"

"Tyonne, I'm sor..."

Tamika cut in. "I'm here too, just so you know. Your best friend, remember? The one you were supposed to be trying to rekindle your relationship with?"

Shatara opened her mouth to respond, but Tyonne chimed back in.

"You and Shatina have been acting real funny, Shatara. We just tried to call her before we called you and now she's not answering. What's up?"

Shatara's mind flashed with all kinds of answers to that question, but she knew she couldn't say anything. It was at that moment that Shatara finally understood her sister.

She had been so mad at Shatina all this time, when her sister was caught up, like she said. Shatara couldn't have foreseen anything that had been happening over the past week or two since she had been kidnapped.

Life was crazy and she owed her sister a huge apology if she ever got the chance to speak with her again.

Shatara swallowed, then put on the performance of a lifetime. "Guys, I'm so sorry. I just needed some time to process. You know I took a leave of absence from school right?"

"Yes," Tyonne said. "Your mom told me while she was in the middle of screaming and threatening me, asking me where you were."

"Me too," Tamika said.

"I'm sorry," Shatara repeated.

"Whatever," Tyonne said. "But what's going on with you? Why did you leave school?"

Shatara chuckled nervously, hoping they bought her next lie. "It's stupid."

"We gathered that," Tamika said. "But how stupid are we talking. Did you do it over a boy, or what?"

"No, not a boy. I was mad at my mom for not letting me study abroad."

Tamika sucked her teeth. "Are you serious? So you scared us half to death over a temper tantrum?"

"Like I said, it was stupid, then I hid out in a hotel because I knew Mom would be pissed. I didn't reach out to you guys because I didn't want you to get in trouble with your parents."

"Tuh, that plan fell through," Tamika said. "My mom and Tyonne's mom interrogated us via FaceTime. We had no clue where you were and they almost didn't believe us."

"Wow." Shatara was at a loss for words.

"Anyway, on to the next subject," Tyonne said. "I finally told my parents I'm pregnant. Are you coming to the baby shower or are you still *in hiding*?"

Shatara ignored the jab as her mind flashed to Sam and her pregnancy.

"Yes, of course I'm coming, Tyonne. I know I owe you both big time."

Chapter 19

Buster watched as Shatara returned from the bathroom carrying her cell phone. He hoped she hadn't let anything slip to her cousin or the crew might be in deep trouble.

Then he relaxed.

Shatara wasn't stupid. She knew how much was at stake here just like everybody else. He opened his mouth to say something when there was a knock at the front door.

"Who is that, Max again?" Sam asked.

Buster had been worried about Max. He had been running around like a chicken with his head cut off trying to find Shatina.

It wasn't Max at the door.

It was Shatina and Sam's man, Robert.

Sam looked confused. "What are you two doing together? Shatina, I thought you..." Her voice trailed off. "What's going on?"

Shatina walked in and looked at Shatara, then Buster, then back at Robert. "I'll let Ted explain."

All eyes were now on Robert, or Ted, as Shatina had called him.

He took the floor. "Listen, I don't have a ton of time to explain but I'm with the police."

Sam gasped as her eyes widened. "You what?"

Robert reached out to grab her hand. "Sam, I'm sorry I didn't tell you. I couldn't. It was my job…"

Sam wrenched away from him and stomped toward her bedroom.

Robert looked at the rest of the group. "Sorry about this," he said, then followed Sam.

Buster looked at Shatina. "How much does he know? What did you tell him?"

Buster felt himself begin to panic internally. He wasn't ready to go to jail.

Shatina tried to calm him. "He doesn't know everything, but I had to tell him about Carmen."

"Shatina!" Buster's eyes widened even more as his body grew hot and cold.

"Listen," she said, putting her hands up. "I have to go find Max. I left my phone at the apartment. I'll be back."

"Wait, wait…" Buster called out to her.

"Shatina!" Shatara said, but her sister was on a mission.

Buster's mind was swimming. Shatina didn't know the plan had moved up to tonight.

"Why would she do that?" he asked, turning to Shatara. "Does she have any idea what kind of trouble she just put us in?"

Shatara shook her head. "I have no idea, Buster, but I trust my sister." She swallowed. "If Shatina told Robert what's going on, that has to mean she believes he can help us. I mean think about it. He's a cop."

That didn't make Buster feel any better.

He didn't want to be selfish, but his life flashed before his eyes. He wouldn't survive life behind prison walls. He imagined Robert coming out of Sam's bedroom, holding her in handcuffs while other cops swarmed in to grab him and Shatara.

Shatara would be let go because she was innocent, and probably Esmeralda too, but the rest of them? They were going down.

Chapter 20

Infuriated wasn't the word.

Sam was livid. Disgusted. Betrayed. How could he?

"Baby, please…" Robert said with tears in his eyes. "I don't have much time to explain but just know I never meant to hurt you."

"Did you know who I was the whole time?" Sam thundered. "Was that why you found me? You reached out to me on that app, pulled me in like you were really interested. We slept together, Robert! I am carrying your child. How could you?"

"Sam, listen. None of that was fake."

She snorted, wiping a bitter tear from her eye. "Oh yeah, and how am I supposed to believe that? You were a cop this whole time. Are you really Max's father?"

Ted paused. "I am Max's father, and yes, I also did know who you were. But I swear, my feelings for you are real."

"So what, you were just using me to try to find information on your son?"

He shook his head, then looked down. "No, it was about Brighton. I knew you two had dealings with each other."

Sam felt like she had been slapped in the face.

Robert's words struck her to the core.

Not only had Brighton played her after finding out about Robert, but Robert had played her the whole time for information about Brighton.

"You're sick!"

Vomit rushed forward through her esophagus, and Sam hurried to the bathroom. Robert held her hair back as she hurled.

"Sick!" she spat again.

Robert watched as she washed her mouth out.

"I never want to see you again," she said when she finished.

"Sam…"

"And I'm reporting you to your superiors. There has to be some rule against impregnating a suspect."

"You weren't a suspect!"

"Was I not? Whatever, Robert. Get the hell out of my house. I can't believe I almost lost my life over you."

Robert tried to say more, but his words fell on deaf ears. Sam was done. She had no idea what this would mean for her and her unborn child growing forward, but whatever it was, she would be ready to face it.

***

Buster and Shatara could hear Sam screaming at Robert from her bedroom, then again in the bathroom.

Shatara's head was spinning. "I can't get over the fact that Sam is dating Max's dad."

Buster shrugged. "She used to date Max too, before she met Robert. She didn't know they were related though."

Shatara gasped. "Really?"

Buster nodded. "It was a whole mess but I'll have to fill you in later."

Now she was curious. "Have you and Sam ever dated?"

Buster's expression changed and he didn't have to answer, but he did. "We did, but we're not messing around anymore. She's all wrapped up in Robert as you can see."

"And what about you?" Shatara felt insecure all of a sudden. "Do you still have feelings for her?"

Buster shook his head. "Not in that way. I'm not the type of guy to dwell on someone who is not interested in me. I can't front, I was feeling her when we messed around, but she made her choice."

Shatara relaxed. "Good," she said, satisfied with that answer.

Buster grew uneasy. "But there is one other thing."

She stared at him. "What?"

He toyed with the string from his sweatpants. "Are you aware of how I know your sister?"

Chapter 21

Shatina grabbed her phone from her apartment and immediately texted Max. *Where are you?*

Seconds later, he responded. *Where are you?*

She texted him a location to meet her and he arrived in less than ten minutes. He stalked up to her car and wrenched her out of the driver's seat, crushing her lips in a kiss. "You have no idea how worried I was," he said when they pulled back.

"I know, I'm sorry," Shatina said. "But I have something to tell you."

"I have a lot to tell you too," he said. "But you first."

Shatina braced herself for his reaction. "It's about Ted."

Max looked like he was thrown for a loop. "My father, Ted? What happened with him?"

Shatina launched into the story.

By the time she finished, Max was numb. His mind had gone in so many directions, he didn't know which way was up. He would have to have a conversation with Ted later, but for now, Shatina had to be informed about the new developments in the plan.

***

Tony stood in the basement of the club with two guns in the back of his waistband, both sporting silencers. He knew his plan was a sloppy one, but desperate times called for desperate measures.

His main goal was freeing Carmen, then the other girls. Everything else would just have to fall wherever it laid.

He looked around for Flex, but it was mostly out of paranoia. Flex was upstairs talking to Brighton. Tony had been sent to do an afternoon round by himself, which meant he would have a few moments to talk to Carmen.

He entered her room and she rushed from the bed to meet him. "Mi amor," she said, then they shared a deep, soulful kiss.

When they pulled back, Tony made his announcement. "I'm getting you out of here tonight."

She gasped in shock, then fear crossed her features. "How?"

Tony swallowed. "I have a plan and some people are helping me from outside."

She searched his eyes. "Who's helping you? How did you put this together so quickly?"

"I had to."

"Tony, are you sure you thought of everything? That man is evil."

"I know he is. Trust me. It's going to be fine."

Tony had made Carmen a lot of promises, and she trusted him, as far as he knew. Deep down in his heart he felt it wasn't fair not to tell her what Brighton had planned for her tonight, but Tony couldn't bear the look on her face when he shared that news.

As he exited her room, he sent up a prayer to God that even if he didn't make it, Carmen made it out of here alive.

***

Max shared with Shatina all the new details of the plan. "Wait, does Ted know what we're going to do?" he asked.

Shatina shook her head. "He knows that Brighton has Carmen, but our conversation got interrupted before I told him anything else."

Max had been filled with anxiety at first, but that statement helped him relax. "Okay, good. Hopefully we can pull this off and then let the chips fall where they may."

A faraway look crossed her features. "I hope so too."

Chapter 22

On our way with the vans.

It was go time. Tony stared at the text from the chat, his body filling with adrenaline. He needed to focus because this plan had to be perfect or it would fail.

Brighton had people in the club setting up a secret silent auction. Rich buyers were coming from all over the country to purchase the girls. Some would be shipped overseas. The thought of Brighton's operation made Tony sick to his stomach though Brighton spoke of it with pride.

He couldn't believe he wanted to be that man's right hand.

Tony couldn't wait to take him down.

There were guards stationed at the back door of the club, in the hallway leading to the basement, plus Flex was going to be in the basement with Tony, guarding the girls so the process would go smoothly.

Brighton had warned everyone in a meeting earlier that day that everyone had to move discreetly because they weren't supposed to be conducting business at the club.

The shooting had caused the main business to be shut down until the police investigation was over.

Tony thought Brighton was full of arrogance to think he could run a whole auction selling all these girls without getting caught. Then again, the man had been trafficking girls for years and no one had suspected him yet.

No time to dwell on that.

Carmen needed to be his only focus.

***

Brighton was preparing for the night of his life. He was about to be almost twenty million dollars richer, minus McConnell and his other contact's cuts.

Once these girls were sold, he needed a vacation. Brighton planned to fly out of the country after the event was over. He already had a private jet and a sexy lady waiting for him. One who fulfilled his needs better than Sam.

Aside from the club being shut down for a while, Brighton needed to reconsider his ties to Blue Street. He loved the power that came with being gang affiliated, plus the extra money that came in from the drugs and guns, but the gang was moving sloppy.

Also, they made a lot of decisions that caused them to look weak.

It seemed that Parker Square would have been the better option with how bodies on Brighton's side had been dropping left and right.

He would think more about that later. Now it was time for him to make this money.

He nodded at McConnell as their guests began to arrive. McConnell nodded back with a smirk. Brighton could practically smell the cash flowing throughout the room.

***

Max and Shatina rode together in one van, while Esmeralda and Slim, Rambo, and Jared drove the other three. The time was almost here.

They arrived at the back of the club without incident.

The guards looked startled at first but didn't have time to react because Jared and Rambo hopped out, ending them immediately.

Max's stomach twisted as their bodies dropped, but he knew what he signed up for tonight. *It's for the greater good,* he reminded himself and sent Tony a text telling him to assemble the girls.

Max hoped this worked quickly because they had to be in and out before anyone noticed.

Jared and Rambo approached the back door with Slim following behind them.

Esmeralda hopped out of the van behind Slim and Max and Shatina were exiting their van when shots rang out from the roof, sending everyone in a panic.

"No!" Max watched in horror as bullets went through Jared and Rambo's heads simultaneously. Slim was also hit in the leg. Esmeralda, Max, and Shatina scrambled back inside their vans. Esmeralda screamed for Slim to get inside, but he was busy shooting back against the shooters on the roof.

She followed suit and they took them out.

One fell off the roof and landed in the middle of the street, while the other guy's body dropped where he stood.

Max was in shock. He couldn't believe he just saw his brother die.

"Max, what are we going to do?" Shatina asked as they watched Esmeralda half-pull a limping Slim back to her van.

They had no way of knowing if there were more shooters on the roof or lurking somewhere else nearby. Tony hadn't mentioned that possibility.

Chapter 23

As soon as Tony got the text, he was ready for action.

He watched Flex go into one of the girl's rooms at the end of the hall. Once he was safely inside, Tony scrambled up the steps, poking his head out the door to see two guards doing a round in the hallway.

He made sure his silencer was secure, took a deep breath, then whipped around into the hallway, shooting them both before he could think.

They went down easily, thank God.

Tony needed to make sure they were dead though. No loose ends.

He crept down the hall, his gun at the ready. One guy was out but the other was still moving. One more bullet finished him off. Then Tony pulled their bodies into a nearby bathroom, closing the door behind him.

After that he poked his head back out into the hall to make sure the coast was clear, then darted back to the basement.

It was almost over.

Carmen would be free soon.

As Tony walked down the stairs to take out Flex, he felt his phone buzzing in his pocket. What was it? He checked the message and his heart dropped.

We've got trouble!

***

Brighton stood at the podium, a huge blank screen behind him ready to display what would be a slideshow prepared for the event. They usually brought the girls out on stage for the audience to bid, but because of recent incidents, they had to increase security.

The pictures would have to suffice.

"Good evening ladies and gentlemen," Brighton started with a smile.

"I'm glad you all came. I'm sure you'll be happy with our selections, but remember, every girl must go tonight. Get ready for the bargain of a lifetime."

Brighton saw one of the men seated at a front table smile.

That gave him the confidence he needed to continue.

He clicked the button in the remote he was holding and the first slide showed on the screen. It was one of their best looking girls. Brighton knew the crowd would go wild over her.

He smirked, knowing exactly how this was about to go down. "How about we start this bid at one million? Any takers?"

Immediately a hand shot up in the back of the room.

Brighton chuckled. "Very well, we have our first bidder. Anybody for one-point-five?"

No one made a move.

"You guys are playing nice today, huh?" Brighton chuckled nervously. He was hoping to make at least three million from that girl. Oh well, he had to move forward.

"No more takers?"

Everyone remained in place.

"Alrighty, sold to the gentleman in the back!"

Brighton looked at McConnell, then clicked the remote to move to the next slide, but before he could utter another word, chaos ensued.

Almost in unison, everyone jumped from their seats, guns drawn in Brighton's direction.

"Freeze! FBI!" the gentleman who purchased the girl shouted.

Brighton blinked in shock. "What? What is this?"

He dropped his clicker remote, held his hands up, and looked at McConnell, his legs trembling.

McConnell's face was red with shame. "Sorry, Brighton."

Chapter 24

Max was scared out of his mind. They were expected to complete the mission, but Jared and Rambo were dead and Slim was leaking. What if there were more shooters? Did Max have the guts to pull this off?

He turned to Shatina. "Do you think we should go in there?"

She shook her head, her face filled with as much shock as he felt. "I don't know. Max, I'm so sorry about your brother."

Max swallowed. His mind was reeling over Jared, but he had to focus.

He sent a text to the chat. *Jared and Rambo are gone. Slim is hit.*

Seconds later, a message came from Sam. *Are you and Shatina okay? What about Esmeralda and Tony?*

Max blinked back tears. He couldn't do this. The one time in his life when he was supposed to come through for someone and he couldn't do it.

He was ashamed to admit that he didn't want to get out of the van and face potential death. Images of Rambo and Jared going down filled his mind.

Shatina took over and answered Sam's questions. *We're okay, but Slim needs medical attention.*

Sorry about your brother, Max, Buster texted.

Max didn't have the strength to text back.

***

Shatina had a horrible feeling about this whole situation. They were all going to die. Her, Max, Esmeralda, and Slim if they didn't do something soon. They had to make a move.

"I'm going out there," she said, and moved to exit the van.

Max pulled her back. "No, you're not. What if there are more shooters?"

"Max, we have to! We can't just sit here and wait for them to come get us!"

Shatina cocked her gun. "Are you coming with me?"

***

Tony didn't know what to think after Max's text, but he didn't have time to dwell on it. He hurried down the hall in the basement and raced into Carmen's room. The plan was to make sure she was the first to get inside a van, then go back and get the other girls.

When he entered her room, however, Tony got the shock of his life.

Flex stood there with a sinister grin, holding Carmen in front of his body, Brighton's machete at her neck.

"Well, well, well. What do we have here?" he said.

"Let her go!" Tony demanded, wondering how Flex knew he was coming to free Carmen.

Flex picked up on his confusion. "I knew you had been acting strange lately," he said. "Leaving at random

123

hours of the day, and always on your phone. You should have been more careful."

Carmen's eyes were wide with fear and it broke Tony's heart.

Flex continued. "I knew you had a thing for Miss Carmen here, so when Brighton told me what he had planned, I told him about your little affair."

"Man I don't care about none of that. Just let her go!"

Flex sneered. "Sorry, I can't do that."

Chapter 25

Sam's house was in a frenzy. "I knew we shouldn't have done this!" She screamed after hearing the news about Jared and Rambo. "Now they're stuck there at that club and there's nothing we can do to help them."

"Call Robert!" Shatara suggested. "The cops can help them."

"That's not going to work," Sam said. "By the time he gets there, they'll be dead."

***

Tony and Flex were at a standstill when footsteps thundered down the hallway. *Finally,* Tony thought, keeping his gun trained on Flex.

It took them long enough, but Shatina and her crew finally arrived.

Only it wasn't Shatina.

"Freeze! FBI!" Tony heard someone scream behind him. "Put the gun and the machete down, now!"

Flex looked just as shocked as Tony felt, but he didn't drop the machete.

Tony didn't drop his gun either.

He would die standing here if he had to, but he wasn't making a move until Carmen was safe.

"I said, drop the weapons!" the agent yelled.

Neither Flex nor Tony made a move.

***

Max not only felt guilty for not being ready to avenge his brother's death immediately, but he also now felt like a coward.

His woman was ready for battle, while he was shaking in his boots.

"Shatina," he said. "You stay here and I'll go."

Her eyes widened. "No, Max! I'm not letting you go out there alone!"

Esmeralda emerged from her van as she spoke, Slim limping behind her. Both of them headed toward the back door.

"Shatina, you have to stay behind. Please. I wouldn't be able to live with myself if something happened to you."

Shatina swallowed. "I can't lose you either."

They kissed briefly, then Shatina sat back as Max exited the van. He rushed to follow Esmeralda and Slim, praying he made the right decision.

No gunshots sounded around them, which put his heart temporarily at ease, but the three of them were startled when the back door of the club banged open and people began pouring outside, a mixture of girls and men and women with guns.

Max raised his gun and one of the men trained his on him. "Freeze! FBI!" he shouted.

Max dropped his weapon, just as Ted came out of the building with Carmen and Tony.

"Stand down!" he commanded the other officer. "That's my son!"

Esmeralda and Slim had already dropped their weapons too, and Esmeralda ran to her sister, practically tackling her with joy.

Tears streamed down both of their cheeks.

Finally, a good moment in this disastrous situation.

Chapter 26

Sam was frantic. Why wasn't anyone answering their phones?

"Turn on the news!" she commanded, and Buster scrambled for the remote.

Panic filled her body as Buster went to the local news station.

Nothing out of the ordinary was showing, but Sam still didn't know what to think. She should have called Robert like Shatara suggested. Maybe he could have helped.

If Max and Shatina were dead, she didn't know what she would do.

"Oh God, please..." She clasped her hands in front of her, squeezing her eyes shut.

"Look!" Shatara said.

Sam opened her eyes to see a *Breaking News* signal on the screen. "Developing news about the recently closed club behind me," the reporter said. "The investigation is still underway, but it appears several people have been arrested, along with multiple fatalities. More developments coming soon."

Sam stood frozen in place as she tried to make out any of the people from the crowd. She couldn't tell if any of them were Max or Shatina.

"Come on, please answer your phones!" she said, and tried one more time.

***

Once the officers ascertained that the crew wasn't a threat, Slim was taken in an ambulance, and Jared and Rambo were hauled away too.

Max, Shatina, Esmeralda, and Tony were taken into custody.

Shatina had no idea what the rest of this night would lead to, but she prayed that whatever happened, this situation was over.

***

Brighton Miller sat in an interrogation room, fuming. He couldn't believe McConnell turned on him. He never saw it coming. All his hopes, dreams, and money, down the drain. His mind began racing, trying to develop a plan.

Just then, the door to the room opened and a man walked in.

It was the same man from the auction, the one who purchased the girl, then arrested Brighton. "Good evening," he said with a smirk. "I don't believe we've been formally introduced." The man extended his hand. "My name is Agent Robert Myles, but you can call me Ted."

Brighton made no move to return the man's greeting. He didn't care who the hell he was, he just wanted out of this place.

"No comments?" Ted said. "Or do you want to call your lawyer?"

129

Brighton scowled when Ted asked that question, causing him to burst out in raucous laughter.

Ted exited the room and Brighton banged his cuffed fists against the table, swearing profusely.

***

Max, Shatina, Esmeralda, and Tony were taken to separate rooms. Shatina didn't know where the women from the club were taken. She was just happy to be alive and praying this all would be over soon.

When the officer came in to question her, she planned to tell the truth and hoped everyone else did the same.

She couldn't have gone through all this just to face life in prison.

Chapter 27

Two weeks later...

All of the crew met at Luke's spot to reconvene. The past couple of weeks had been hectic to say the least. When Max's parents heard the news about their son, they disowned him.

It hurt, but not as much as he thought it would because it wasn't like they had a stellar relationship before this anyway.

The city was in a frenzy with all kinds of gossip flying around about what went on that night at the club.

It was the second set of shootings in less than two weeks, and the club was supposed to have been shut down.

Of course, the streets knew about some of the activity that went on despite the club's status.

Finally, a major part of the story broke. Brighton Miller's face was plastered on every station and his identity as a crooked politician who was also a sex trafficker, murderer, and drug and gun dealer emerged. The women that he had held as prisoners were released to their families.

The media had a field day, especially since the FBI revealed that they had been after Brighton for years.

Max thought it was the irony of ironies that his long-lost biological father was the head of the case. That part of the story wasn't leaked to the news though. Ted's boss was the one who held all interviews with the media since Ted was undercover in his role.

Max still wasn't sure what to think about him. Ted was his father, yes, and the only living relative who seemed to want anything to do with him, but he wasn't sure he could be trusted.

Granted, Ted was in the middle of working out an immunity deal for the crew, having them testify against Brighton for their freedom, but still. Ted had been lying all along about who he was. Max pushed thoughts of kindling a father-son relationship with him out of his mind.

The focus now was on convincing Slim to testify if they were granted the deal.

"Come on, Slim," Shatina was saying. "If we get this deal, we can be done with the situation for good."

Slim shook his head. "I ain't no snitch, Ma."

Max jumped in. "You wouldn't do it for your boys? Brighton was down with Blue Street. Jared and Rambo were down with Parker Square. Where is your loyalty?"

Slim wasn't moved. "I hear what you're saying, and you know I'm messed up about what happened but still. There's rules to this game and certain lines I can't cross."

***

Finally, it was time for the trial. Shatina hoped this would be a speedy process. Her life was in an uproar, but the one good thing from it all was that her and Max were safe, at least for the time being, and her and Shatara seemed to be on good terms.

Shatina sat in a room with Max, Esmeralda, and Carmen, waiting for the trial to begin. Tony was supposed to testify too as well as the rest of the women from the club. Tony was being transported from the jail, where he was being kept because of his involvement in the Blue Street gang and Brighton's organization.

Shatina's breath caught in her throat as Ted entered the room.

It was time.

She stood, but his expression gave her pause.

"What is it?" she asked, her heart dropping to her knees.

"We requested a continuance," Ted explained. "Tony was found dead in his cell, and McConnell is missing."

Carmen screamed and Shatina's mind went blank.

They had found out through Ted previously that McConnell had been flipped by the FBI over a year ago and he was helping them build a case against Brighton.

Now that he was gone and Tony was dead, Shatina didn't know what she was going to do.

Chapter 28

Finally, there was a turnaround.

After a long, arduous trial, Brighton Miller was sentenced to life in prison. Originally, the death penalty was on the table, but since McConnell wasn't as forthcoming with his testimony as he promised and Tony was murdered, the prosecutor had to go with the next best option.

The police had caught up with McConnell as he tried to flee the country. He went through his own trial after Brighton's and he was sentenced to ten years.

Max, Shatina, and the rest of the crew were granted immunity, but Slim refused to testify.

Ted worked out a deal for him because of his involvement in helping to save the girls, so he was only given two years and community service.

It seemed that the battle was finally over. Shatina felt like she could breathe again.

While the trial was going forth, she fought through her senior year of college.

Shatara did the same, and their parents were excited to learn that the twins were set to graduate.

***

Sam and Robert had a long way to go, but they reached an understanding after months of arguing back and forth.

Robert had forgiven Sam for cheating with Brighton, but Sam couldn't shake the fact that he played her for information on Brighton.

"How do I know that I could ever fully trust you?" she asked.

"Baby I swear, I will resign from my position and stick with teaching. Whatever it takes, all I want is you and our daughter."

That was their final conversation and Sam told him she would think about it.

One night she called him over, telling him she made a decision.

He arrived less than a half hour later to see Sam in a pink nighty, her baby bump fully evident.

They made love that night and since then, things weren't perfect, but they had come a long way.

Their beautiful baby girl, Nevaeh, was born on time and healthy.

***

Surprisingly to some, but not to others, Buster and Shatara were hitting things off nicely. They had been getting to know one another for the better part of the past year, but neither of them seemed to be ready to make the move necessary to take it to the next level.

That was until Buster showed at her dorm one night with a bouquet of red roses. "Will you be mine?" he asked in a seductive voice.

135

Shatara was shocked that he traveled to see her, but filled with joy. She happily obliged and they had been going steady ever since.

Chapter 29

Max and Shatina had been through the worst ordeal imaginable but it seemed that their troubles were finally over.

Brighton was in prison, no one else was blackmailing them, and life was starting to come together. Max had enrolled in tech school, an idea he previously flirted with, but wasn't sure he could do it.

Shatina was beyond proud of her man and the fact that he was turning around for the better.

They visited Jared and Rambo's graves with the rest of the crew on the anniversary after their deaths. It was a bittersweet moment, but Shatina was glad the rest of the crew was still standing.

Despite a whole year passing, Max's parents still weren't speaking to him. That hurt him, Shatina knew, especially since her parents had readily forgiven her indiscretions, just happy she was okay.

Ted had been reaching out, but Max barely returned his calls. Shatina knew he wanted to build a relationship with his father but didn't know how.

When Shatina's parents learned that she was dating Max, they were livid. They rejected him and threatened to have him arrested if he ever came near their home.

Shatina knew why they felt that way but she wanted their approval. They had no idea who Max really was, what kind of man he had become since they had been together.

Many times, when Shatina was down, Max was the one to lift her. When she felt like giving up, Max was there to ease her burdens.

Shatina resolved to give it time.

Her parents would come around one day.

When graduation rolled around, her parents were cordial toward Max, then when he got down on one knee in front of them at the restaurant, Shatina could have sworn her father was going to have a heart attack.

"Shatina," Max had said with tears in his eyes. "You're the only woman I've ever truly loved. I've never met anyone else like you. You're beautiful, intelligent, and you've had my back through thick and thin. I couldn't imagine spending my life with anyone else but you if you'll have me. Babe, will you marry me?"

Shatina's eyes filled and she knew her parents would hate her decision, but there was no way she would say no. She accepted, and everyone in the restaurant outside of her parents erupted in applause.

Even Tyonne and Tamika were *Team Max*, after Shatina and Shatara held a lengthy conversation with them.

Tyonne had a baby boy, Sherron, and when she first mentioned his name on FaceTime, Shatina and Max shared a long laugh.

"What's so funny?" Tyonne demanded. "Don't make fun of my baby's name!"

"We're not," Shatina said. "Max's birth name was Sherron."

"Yeah, I'm thinking of changing it back too, since my parents disowned me," Max joked.

Tyonne rolled her eyes. "Oh, brother. You two are too much for me."

***

After graduation, Tyonne and Tamika moved back home, as did Shatara. The girl's bond continued to strengthen, and baby Sherron was spoiled by all his aunties.

Chapter 30

Esmeralda and Carmen had been living with Luke since Carmen was freed, but Carmen was ready to branch out on her own. She learned design on the internet and began creating different pieces to sell at her own boutique.

Luke and Esmeralda were still going steady, and he helped Carmen apply for a grant. After that, she was ready to set up shop.

Esmeralda was beyond proud of her sister. Tony's death had left a scar on Carmen's heart, but she seemed to be healing through her creative endeavors.

Esmeralda also had plans for the future.

Ever since she helped save her sister from Brighton Miller, she became fascinated with the FBI. During the trial, she had several conversations with Ted.

He agreed to give her a good recommendation if she got through the police academy.

Esmeralda's tenacity never faltered and she graduated top of her class.

She started off as a beat cop, but Ted told her that there would be a promising career for her in a few years.

***

Ted and Max were still working on their relationship. Ted had come to Shatina's apartment to visit a few times since Max had moved in, and Max and Shatina had gone to Ted's house a few times too.

Max was slowly opening up to his father, and Ted was happy their bond was finally beginning to form.

***

The day finally came for Max and Shatina's wedding. Three years after the Brighton Miller situation had ended, and everyone was thriving.

After Max graduated from tech school, he and Buster opened a business together, focusing on digital investigations.

Sam opened her salon. Being a mom kept her busy, but she stopped in a few days a week to help out, though she left most of the work to her appointed manager.

Shatina and Shatara were closer than ever, Shatina's parents had finally accepted Max, and Ted and Max found common enjoyment in videogame tournaments against each other.

The entire crew was present at the wedding.

Max stood at the altar with the pastor, while Shatina walked down the aisle in her white handcrafted dress from Carmen's boutique, arm in arm with her father.

The dress was etched with a flowery design, it had a small train, and Shatina wore her hair pinned up with a long veil that flowed behind her as she walked.

The wedding was held outside since it was summer time, and the sky was clear and blue. Not a cloud in sight.

The two recited handwritten vows, then shared a kiss that left tears in the eyes of all who were present.

Everyone had a great time at the reception, then it was time for Max and Shatina's honeymoon to the Virgin Islands.

"Take care of my daughter now!" Shatina's father joked.

"And make sure you watch out for my son too!" Ted clapped back.

Everyone shared a laugh, then Shatina and Max climbed into their limo, riding off into the sunset.

The End

Dear Reader,

I hope you enjoyed this jam-packed finale to the **Quiet Ones** series. I had no idea Shatina's story would take the form that it did, but I'm glad she found happiness with her nemesis-turned-lover, Max.

Want to read another thriller? Have no fear, I have plenty for you!

Check out Priscilla and Raheem's story in Not What It Seems: A Christian Romance Thriller.

Until next time,

Tanisha Stewart

Before you go...

If you enjoyed *The Enemy You Know*, I would absolutely love to hear your feedback. Please leave a **rating** or **review** commenting on your overall thoughts.

In addition, if you would like access to exclusive updates, giveaways, and more, join my email list at tanishastewartauthor.com/contact.

God bless you, and happy reading!

Tanisha Stewart

PS: If you would like to connect with me on social media, here's where you can find me:

Facebook: Tanisha Stewart, Author
Facebook group: Tanisha Stewart Readers
Instagram: tanishastewart_author
TikTok: authortanishastewart
Twitter: TStewart_Author
YouTube: Tanisha Stewart

Tanisha Stewart's Books

Even Me Series
Even Me
Even Me, The Sequel
Even Me, Full Circle

When Things Go Series
When Things Go Left
When Things Get Real
When Things Go Right

For My Good Series
For My Good: The Prequel
For My Good: My Baby Daddy Ain't Ish
For My Good: I Waited, He Cheated
For My Good: Torn Between The Two
For My Good: You Broke My Trust
For My Good: Better or Worse
For My Good: Love and Respect
Rick and Sharmeka: A BWWM Romance

Betrayed Series
Betrayed By My So-Called Friend
Betrayed By My So-Called Friend, Part 2
Betrayed 3: Camaiyah's Redemption
Betrayed Series: Special Edition

Phate Series
Phate: An Enemies to Lovers Romance
Phate 2: An Enemies to Lovers Romance
Leisha & Manuel: Love After Pain

The Real Ones Series
Find You A Real One: A Friends to Lovers Romance
Find You A Real One 2: A Friends to Lovers Romance
Janie & E: Life Lessons

The Quiet Ones Series
Should Have Thought Twice: A Psychological Thriller
Fooled Me Once: A Psychological Thriller
Never Saw Me Coming: A Psychological Thriller
Reap What You Sow: A Psychological Thriller
Surprise Surprise: A Psychological Thriller
The Enemy You Know: A Psychological Thriller

Standalones
A Husband, A Boyfriend, & a Side Dude
In Love With My Uber Driver
You Left Me At The Altar
Where. Is. Haseem?! A Romantic-Suspense Comedy
Caught Up With The 'Rona: An Urban Sci-Fi Thriller
#DOLO: An Awkward, Non-Romantic Journey Through Singlehood
December 21st: An Urban Supernatural Suspense
Everybody Ain't Your Friend: An Urban Romance Thriller
The Maintenance Man: A Twisted Urban Love Triangle Thriller
Not What It Seems: A Christian Romance Thriller
Vengeance Is Mine: A Psychological Thriller

www.ingramcontent.com/pod-product-compliance
Lightning Source LLC
Chambersburg PA
CBHW060930140726